ABOUT THE AUTHOR

Joel Rose's first novel, *Kill the Poor*, spent four months on the *Voice Literary Supplement* bestseller list. He is also the author of *La Pacifica*, a graphic novel, and the graphic nonfiction *The Big Book of Thugs*. His journalism has appeared in the *New York Times*, *New York* magazine, *New York Newsday*, and various other publications. His screenplay *Dead Weekend* was produced in 1995; and he has written for several television shows, including *Miami Vice* and *Kojak*. He was also an editor at D.C. Comics where he wrote stories for both the *Superman* and *Batman* comic strips.

Joel Rose has been awarded grants from the National Endowment for the Arts and the New York Foundation for the Arts. He established and edited the legendary literary magazine *Between C & D*, which will be relaunched in Autumn 1997. He lives in New York City.

Also by Joel Rose
KILL THE POOR

Kill Kill Faster Faster

Joel Rose

This edition first published in the UK in 1997 by
Rebel Inc., an imprint of Canongate Books,
14 High Street, Edinburgh EH1 1TE

First published in USA in 1997 by Crown Publishers Inc.

British Library Cataloguing-in-Publication Data
A catalogue record for this book is available upon request
from the British Library.

ISBN 0 86241 697 3

Typeset in Fournier by Falcon Oast Graphic Art, East Sussex
Printed and bound by Caledonian International, Bishopbriggs

For my daughters, Céline and Chloé

Birds do it. Bees do it. Let's do it.

Gary Gilmore

I been shot.
I been shot in the head. In the heart.
I been shot in the cheek. In the jaw. In the mouth.
I been shot in the gut.
I been shot in the back, in the arm, in the neck.
I been shot in the balls.

My daughters, my daughters.
My twin daughters.
I'm telling you the truth when I tell you there's

nothing I wouldn't do for them.

Nothing I wouldn't do for my daughters.

You grow up where I grew up, you wonder what's in store for you. You wonder where you'll wind up, what you're going to see.

The way I see it, it's a father's duty—a man's duty— to impart knowledge to his children.

Still, forgive me for what I done.

The city. The city made me do it.

The sun is out, but my side of the street is in shadow. Know what I mean?

If you ask me, Is this a confessional? Yeah, this is a confessional.

I got out of jail, ninth of September 1996, after serving seventeen and a half years of a fifteen-years-to-life sentence. I did my time at Attica, Dannemora, Stormville, Sing Sing, Elmira. Finally where I got out from was Auburn. I walked out of the Auburn lockup. Stood under the stone walls. The 5 and 20, looking down the big boulevard.

You know what the payoff was, man? The payoff was nothing. There was no nothing there. Just a limo.

A big black one.

The ground is falling away. You need help. You know you need it. You reach out your hand.

It's like having it cut off at the wrist, man. It's like having your friggin hand lopped off right there at the payoff.

You ain't stupid, man. You put out your hand, but then you pull it back. So you deny them. You deny them that.

And then what do they have? They have nothing. They have fucking nothing, and you have your name.

My name is Joey One-Way.

What's yours?

But people don't know.

They don't know.

My mother-in-law used to say those exact words. People don't know, Joey. They don't know.

To me, the cardinal rule of child rearing is watch your ass.

My daughters. My poor beautiful daughters. What have I done to them?

This is before I went away. They're like four. Four years old. I used to call them Vile and Bile, the Piss-off Twins. I come to their room. One of them's lying on the floor. I don't even remember which one. There's a carpet, but it's thin and the floor is hard. I say, Man, why you do that shit to your mother? And she say, the one who's doing the talking, she say, What I do?

You hurt her, I said.

No, I din't.

Yes, you did.

On and on like that. Like I had some responsibility. I the father, speaking up for the mother.

I don't have no responsibility. I'm lost. I'm lost in the ionosphere. Don't be coming at me.

Don't be coming at me with that shit.

It ain't pretension or preclusion, none of that shit, but when the needle used to go in my arm, the edge came off, everything go away. I know it ain't doing me no good to think like that, the limo right there in front of me. Still and all, I'm thinking, you know what I'm saying?

I been shot, man. I been shot.

In the gut. Twicet in the head.

In the balls.

Doc says I can still have kids.

But like I'm telling you, I already got kids.

There's a little girl on the sofa. She my girl. My daughter. I'm responsible for her. She's one of the ones. One of the two. The two the twins. The one take down her pants. She touch her vagina. She say, Daddy, when I make pee-pee my vulva stings.

Man, it smells feisty down there.

I say you got to wipe yourself better, baby.

When I used to take the dope from the foil, put it in the cooker, I believed that was the real thing.

If it were to go up my nose, it wouldn't have been the same. It wouldn't have been nothing to my mind.

When it come inside me through the vein, and then go back out through my eyes, through my ears, into the brain, direct hit, from the TV, no matter how fucked up I was, that's what I don't want. Life is tough. Life, it go round and round.

I'm doing battle. I ain't give up. Day after day. There ain't no stopping me really. I accept my fate. Whatever it is, I ain't scared. I always said I'd die young. Leave a good-looking corpse. I ain't young no more, but I ain't no corpse neither.

You give a kid life, all innocent, and what do you get?

I'll tell you:

You get to watch your baby.

You get to watch your baby's fear.

You get to watch your baby's fear grow and grow.

I remember.

I remember my wife. I remember her like it was yesterday.

Our daughters was giving her a hard time. She hated when I stuck my nose in their business, between them and her, but finally I could take it no longer and I stepped in in spite of myself. I said to them, they was just little ones, I said to them, Why do you treat your mother like that? And the two of them looked at me, and then looked at her, and without batting a eye or breaking off their stare, they said, Because she don't fight back.

Let me tell you something.

A male in a house of females. The deed is done by the setting sun.

The truth of it is, really, even if you don't expect nothing from yourself, you expect everything from your children. You expect better than you got.

So like I say, if you ask me, Is this a confessional? Yeah, this is a confessional.

It's not like one or two people are disturbed around us in our society, it's like everybody's disturbed. Know what I'm saying?

Nowadays, it's like everything's out of focus on the street on a rainy night.

I got too much to lose to be walking too slow.

I won't let nobody grab me.

All them years lost.

Man oh man.

I don't know.

I don't know.

Cause for whatever reason, my mind, I'm fucked, man. I'm thinking how Kim's family didn't even bury her properly.

She never would have wanted to be put in the cold, cold ground. They should have burnt her up. That's what she would have wanted. Burn her up good. Her ashes spread under a tree. In some vacant lot or something.

Man, look at me. All of a sudden I'm like a fucking critic of funerals.

Man, don't that beat all.

I stood in my cell at the proper time. A moment of silence, out of respect.

Man, I was bluto.

Bluto with grief.

Hey, I don't speak for no one but myself. I ain't no everyman. I'm more like no man.

No man on every occasion.

You been out there—who am I?

And I'm scared, man . . .

I'm scared.

What I done?

What I done?

I don't remember. I don't fucking remember. Seventeen and a half years away and I'm a fucking blank.

In my eyes it seems like I got the ability to see the old person in everybody. What that person'll be when they grow old and older, what they'll become. Even the youngest, littlest girls on the street. My own daughters. I see them old. I see them buried.

I had a dream.

I been shot.

They had shot me.

They had shot me, but they hadn't killed me.

They should have killed me, but they didn't.

They should have shot me and killed me and put me out of my misery.

But, to tell you the truth, I'm not miserable. That's the thing with me—I'm not miserable.

It's the anger, man.

The red haze. Come down over my brain. The anger.

That's the thing—*the anger*.

The red haze.

And what am I angry about?

You know, I don't have a clue.

Not a clue.

Or I ain't talking.

One or the other.

I owned Flowers's cunt.

I owned it.

I could make it do anything. It was never like that shit, Jane Brody writing about human sexuality in the *New York Times*, or Dr. Ruth or Dr. Judy on the radio.

I owned it.

I would just put my fingers up her cunt, touch the top, you know, push up there, and, after a while, move my fingers down, touch the bottom, put pressure down there.

Then I slide my fingers up, around, touch the wall,

come back down, you know, lick there, you know.

I didn't have to stick my cock in.

I would, but I didn't have to.

I could do it with my hand. She came like a man. Her cunt would erupt. There would be like a gurgling sound, and there'd be like palpitations. Liquid would come. She had a smell. Man, I dug it. When I buried my nose down there and I smelled that smell, I couldn't get enough of it.

It's the street, man, it's the fucking street.

It done it to me.

I been shot.

The bullet caught me in the back, by the kidney. It spun me around.

Beware, motherfucker, someone coming after you, wants to do you dirty.

A robber at your door.

What's he aim to take? What can he take? Your life? Big fucking deal. Your life ain't nothing.

A predator lurks.

He's waiting.

He's waiting for me.

Springing.

Through the door he come before it can close behind.

I make no bones about it.

My daughters scared, terrified, them lying in bed in their room, listening to me and their mother making love, Kim screaming, them not knowing what it was, coming, running, afraid.

I am out of control, man.

My body is shaking.

My mind is not working.

My days are numbered.

There is that red haze.

I owned Flowers's cunt.

I used to ask her, later on, when I was completely fucked, I used to ask her, Am I in a love affair with you or what? And if I am, what the fuck you think you're doing fucking with me like you are? You're fucking with me, right?

It's the not knowing that eats you up. You been there. You know. Right?

Nobody treats me that way. Nobody, I told her. Not like that.

Fuck you, she says.

Fuck you.

Right back.

We all have our own little temptations. That I have fallen is no fault of my own. I'm weak. People say how I'm like so strong, so bad. Bad boy. Women draping over me. Oh, Joey, you look so young. Prison must have agreed with you, ha-ha.

But I'm not young.

I'm old. I'm an old soul.

Flowers called me old man.

She called me knucklehead.

She called me coolman.

She say, Look out.

Women say, Ooh, look out. He's dangerous. He's angry. Careful of Joey One-Way.

One night, it was our last night together, we was in a

hotel, me and Flowers, I accuse her, accuse her of slumming with me, fucking with me, being into me for the sex, for the danger, like she think she better than me.

I'm just playing with her, but she must have thought about it all serious like, took me at my word, because she get all quiet, slip into the bathroom, take a piss, I can hear the tinkle, start dressing for me.

That night, by this time, it's very late. By right she should be home with her husband, Markie Mann, man who got me out of the lockup after all them years, but she's in the hotel bathroom, getting ready to fuck me.

The door is open a crack. I can see her. Fleur. Flower in French.

I call her Flowers.

She comes out. She must have been thinking about it, what I say, it must have been eating at her. She strike a pose. She says, You say I'm slumming with you and you may be right, maybe I am slumming with you. But you like it like that, don't you? You like what I can give you. You like the restaurants, the hotels, the clothes from Agnes B., the scotch I pour you, the Armagnac, the meals with good French cheese. You like being out of the joint, fucking a beautiful woman.

Like that's the criterion.

But she right. She right.

It was an hour before dawn. It was still dark outside. There was no light. Not outside. Not inside. I got up. I had no choice. I couldn't sleep. I couldn't lie there no longer. I was fucked, man. I was fucked. Waiting, knowing, waiting for the cops to arrive. Next to me, all around me, in the big room, big as a fieldhouse, I could hear the men in rows, snoring, men on cots, heads thrown back, necks exposed, like with a straight razor you could do considerable damage.

The night before I been prowling the street.

What I done to her?

The night before I been prowling the street, pacing the city, Friday night, nowhere to go, back and forth, I see sitting in a row, Indian file, outside the parochial school on Avenue B, a long line of old women bundled, waiting, Friday night, lined up for food to be given out the next morning, all night long waiting there, even in the cold.

Me checking out the old dope scene, just for old times' sake, just see the scene, C and D, coke and dope, don't do nothing about scoring.

That's what I'm telling myself.

There was a guy smoking a cigarette in front of a shop on Seventh Street between First and A. The halfway's on Third. A very attractive young girl, maybe seventeen, was coming down Seventh from the opposite direction. The guy with the cigarette put what's left of the butt down on a garbage can lid, let it burn there for a second, watching the girl come. She passed. He kept watching her. His eyes stuck.

I took his butt, man.

I took it. Pick it up, and start smoking it.

See what I'm saying, what I'm driving at?

There's nothing I'm below.

He reach for it, nothing there, probably thought it fell on the ground or something. But I was smoking it, thinking about her, Fleur, flower in French, my baby.

I got out of jail ninth of September 1996 after serving a jolt of seventeen and a half years of a fifteen-to-life, walking out of the Auburn reformatory in Auburn, New York.

People call me Joey One-Way. They call me that because in the joint I used to say, There's only one way I'm getting out of here, and that's in a box.

I warned Flowers. I warned her. Stay the fuck away from me, girl. Please. Stay away.

I told her I was going to write about her, but I told her,

I'm only going to take one aspect of you to write about.

What aspect is that? she asked.

Your cunt, you cunt.

Violence is all around me. What made me so fucking violent? So angry? What is that?

I try to go straight, man. I try. But there's no way. The red haze has taken over.

Not for nothing I don't see nothing. God save me, O my brothers. God save me.

This is what happened to me in the lockup. This is the God's honest truth. There was a lot of shit going down in there. A lot of power and racial shit, blacks, whites, browns, what have you. A lot of slip-sliding, side-stepping, apricot-brandying.

In the lockup, whites are worst, man, hands down. The white man in the joint is the low end of the feeding chain. Not for nothing, the craziest, most irrational, most desperate fucks are the white men.

I'm a white man, man. I'm a white motherfucker. I'm a tough-ass, don't-mess, kick-your-coolie, take-it-in-the-ear, take-no-prisoners, tough-ass, white-butt, swallow-me-whole motherfucker, man.

And I'm not just spouting shit to convince myself neither, motherfucker. I'm not trying to convince you. So don't be saying that shit at me. Don't be thinking it! I'm in your face, cocksucker.

One day in the shower room, I ain't been there in the lockup too long, but I been warned, I been warned, they coming for me. I heard there was some kind of auction on the yard, and I been auctioned off for a couple of packs of cigarettes and now the dirty white boys, the buttfuckers, they coming for me and they want me to know they coming, no bones about it, and they want me to know I am theirs, which I do.

This is the story I tell Fleur when she ask. This is what I tell her. It is like a seduction dance. This is how it was when I was the fresh meat, my love.

She commiserate, sweet thing. She tell me she know all about it, she been there, done that. After all, she tell me, she been in prison in Marseilles.

Surprise, surprise.

I look at her, see what I see, but when I look deep, I don't know what she know. I know she telling me the truth, but I don't know what she went through being in prison in France. Did they serve her pâté? You know what I'm saying?

What I know is what I know, and what I know is they was coming and nobody was looking out for me, and I didn't ask nobody to look out for me and I didn't look for nobody, everybody out for themselves and no one was asking, survival of the fittest. I'd been doing my best, talking tough, but only when necessary, keeping to myself, trying to stay out of the general flow of it. You hear the rap, you seen the movie. You know. You gotta do something crazy to keep them off you, man. Make them think you one crazy motherfucker. Then once you do that, then everybody stays away, cause they think, that dude . . . you know, he crazy, man, he crazed. Still and all, I'm living in fear. Pure fear. And I'll tell you another thing, I never told nobody, I never breathed a word, not to a soul, what I done, killed a sister, that my wife, my Kimba, was a sister. You better believe I never told nobody that. They woulda been writing on my tombstone dead by dawn. Bet your bottom dollar on that one, bro, them black men woulda been the ones coming for me, woulda grabbed me by the short hairs, and hold me up to the light. Why you marrying a black woman, brother? You got deep-seeded trouble with black women? You don't like black women? You marrying a black woman so you can kill her? Is that it, bro? You trying to inflict you white ass on a black woman, brother? Is that it?

So I'm in the shower, and I don't mind saying like I said, I'm scared, I'm scared all the time, and I'm watching my ass all the time, and a bunch of these greasy-haired nancy boys, these fucks, these buttfuckers, they come for me. They're not there for nothing, they're there for me, they come to do me specific. Two or three of them grab me and the head buttfucker, no questions asked, just bend me over and sticks his cock up my ass. Plenty of grease up here, he says, make me stand right up straight on the end of it, pain, shock, fear, make me suddenly jerk my hand away where one of his partners in crime got me by the wrist, and I reach underneath, between my legs, and I grab the guy who's got his cock up my ass by the balls, at first almost like a caress, and he respond real low and sexy and breathy, That's right, and I just yank as hard as I fucking can, and I mean I yank, and I tear his balls out by the fucking roots, breathy, you hear what I'm saying, by the fucking roots!

Oh, man, he howling. The man he writhing and howling, and all bloody between the legs, his nuts hanging in my hand, his scrotum. He collapses on the floor. Everybody's looking, staring, nobody saying nothing, waiting to see what I'm gonna do. The guy's screaming. Man, you gotta love agony. Agony in others is a first love. That's the thing. That's cool. Can't help your enjoyment, man, the guy'd just been fucking you brutal up the ass, now lying at your feet, rolling on the floor, crying, you know what I'm saying, and when he fell to the tile floor it was like a relief on my sphincter, daddy, you hear me when I tell you, like someone took a cork out my ass, I don't know why, and I just relax, I just let go, I let fly, and I shit him. I shit him, right square on his ugly fucking buttfucker face, where he deserve.

In my own defense, I'd had to take a shit anyway. All that time, when I was standing in the shower before it all came down, I was washing myself, I was thinking, man, I got to get out of here and take a shit, but I hate it when you're all wet and the toilet paper get all soggy and stick on your asshole, so I decide I'm gonna hold it till after, and then this guy comes in, this pale white-skinned buttfucker nancy boy with his cock in his hand, all purple and red and stiff and skinny-minny, and he think he slick and he bungie-hole me, he do, him lying on the tile floor between my legs now, whimpering, Oh, oh, my balls, my balls, what you do to my balls, sweet Jesus! and it just come over me and I just let go my sphincter on him. I shit him right then and there.

Shit went in his mouth, up his nose, in his eyes. The release was like pure pleasure. Seeing all that nasty there on his face, the guy gagging and retching and coughing, I bent right down there over him, and I kneeled over him and I talked to him in whispers, take my revenge, tough guy, and he could hear me even through the pain and shit, and I scoped out his friends, and I pinched his fucking nostrils while I stared at them, like a fucking sado lover, get his attention, look down at him, make him look in my eyes, make him come better, rise to the heights, you know, pinched them flaring nostrils off, and I clamped my hand over his slash mouth like we was into rough sex, the two of us, the stink of my shit getting to him, saints be praised, you know how it is, you know what they say, my shit don't stink, and out of the blue, just like that, he start to throw up, you know, retch, and heave real violent, deep from within, his fish-white belly going up and down, doing a dance, heaving, so I almost feel bad for him, almost feel compassion, you hear what I'm saying? As far as I was concerned, I had made my point, the hard-boys, his posse, no one making a move, me thinking they know who I am now, I home free, and I got up, I took pity, yes I did, I got up, feeling magnacious, and begin to walk away from the poor fuck lying on the floor at my feet covered with my shit and his throw-up.

And at the door of the shower a big tall black guy who been watching, a big tall guy leaning on a mop, he been watching, and it finally dawns on me, it because of him the dirty white boys ain't made a move on me and he stops me, he says to me, Don't walk away from that shit, man. You walk away from a situation like that, that man come back at you, he kill you. You don't last till six o'-clock.

I look at the guy talking to me. He got sort of like gentle liquid eyes. Brown, soft, kindly. And I see what he say to me is the truth, come from the bottom of his heart, from what he knows, from his well. He looking at me, deep at me, making a connection, not wanting me to miss what he telling me.

So I take what the black man say to heart, and I turn back to finish what I started. The nancy boy's still on the floor, his pants down around his ankles, a puddle of blood under his ass, his cock hanging crooked on his thigh, foreskin all aquiver, a poor little pathetic pink dunce cap, limp little cock, you call that a cock, motherfucker?, shrunken up, no good no more to nobody. His buddies looking at me, looking at the black guy.

I stare back at them. This time there ain't gonna be no loving. I clamp his mouth shut, I pinch his nostrils tight, shit and vomit, aroma of stink-stink, and I hold it, and I clamp it, and I pinch it, him choking, him gagging, him sucking that shit and upchuck down into his lungs, gurgle, gurgle, fighting for air, fighting for breath, gurgle, aspirating like nobody's business, gurgle, no one saying a word, not one thing, all silent, his best buds, his good pals, his fellow buttfuckers, watching it happen, doing nothing, just watching. Gurgle. Gurgle. The man shudder. He bellow. Shudder again.

His body arc.

Then that's the end. He expirate, whatever.

Everybody look at him, look at me. No one says nothing. Walk away.

Made my rep. Made me.

After that everybody know Joey One-Way.

Only one way I getting out of here, bro, is in a box.

Everybody respect me when I say that.

Say, Right on, dude.

Joey, man.

Joey.

O my brothers.

J

oey.

Joey. Joey.

Some people are great.

Are born to greatness.

Others have greatness thrust upon them.

Some people are miserable.

Are born miserable.

Others have misery thrust upon them.

Or take it upon themselves.

Joey made himself miserable.

Joey didn't have to be miserable.

Joey could have been on top of the world. Joey had it made. But Joey liked it that way. Liked to be miserable.

Thought he deserved nothing less.

The door opened.

The door opened into a kingdom. It was a secret kingdom.

Joey was standing inside a cage and the cage was scary and there was no way out, but then the door opened and Joey walked out from the cage, through the door, into the sunshine. A limousine was waiting. The driver got out.

He said, Mr. One-Way?

Joey said, Yeah?

The driver came around the big black car. He opened the back door for Joey. He didn't care that Joey just got out of prison, or if he did, he didn't say anything. Joey stood there.

The driver said, Get in. It's okay.

Joey got in.

The driver closed the door behind him, got in his own self.

The driver said, There's coffee there.

Joey said, You got anything stronger?

What do you want?

What do you got?

Anything your heart desires.

Some alcohol would be nice. I haven't had no real alcohol in a long time. Some scotch would be nice. Looking around. You got any scotch back here?

Joey was feeling no pain by the time the car reached the city, by the time the limo got off of the Palisades and across the George Washington Bridge and was on the West Side Highway, heading south, downtown. It's not that he had drank so much or that it showed. He hadn't drank so much and it didn't show. Joey was just Joey.

Fucking Joey.

Joey One-Way.

Out of the joint.

On his way.

The driver pulled up to the docks off of Twelfth Avenue. The driver came around the car, opened the door, said, Go in. They're waiting.

Joey got out. He looked out on the water. Across the river, past the pilings, he saw New Jersey. He went inside.

A receptionist was sitting there. She smiled at him. Nice enough. Nice looking with long legs she knew were hers, liked to show. She said, Yes? She said sweetly, Can I help you? Joey introduced himself. He said, I'm Joey One-Way. Markie Mann told me to come here. I— She lit up, grinned even more broadly, Yes, how do you do? Joey One-Way! We've been expecting you.

The office suddenly full of other young women with long legs too, scurrying around, stealing looks at him. Everybody aware who he is, looking at him when he say his name, when she say his name, say who he is. The sweet receptionist make him feel comfortable, ask him do he want some coffee, a Coke? She buzz Markie on the intercom for him, listen, then say, So sorry, his assistant says he stuck on the set, she says he'll be here as soon as he can, he's expecting you, but she'll be right out to bring you back, show you around, make you at home.

A few seconds later Markie's assistant emerge from the inner sanctum, yet another beauty with long legs, big chest, fashionable clothes. Markie surround himself with babes, Joey guess. She smile, shake his hand, say, Hey, how are ya, how ya feeling, how was your trip, everything all right? She don't let go of his hand, smiling at him, looking in his eyes, assessing, taking the measure of the man, of Joey One-Way. She say, Congratulations. (On getting out?) Take him inside, show him what was to be his office. Say, You want to sit behind the desk? (He didn't.) Went over briefly and informally what he would have to do. Script doctor. Spice up dialogue. Assured him nothing was going to be too heavy for him the first day, or even the first week, relax, take it easy, get used to it.

Joey say, That's cool.

She say, If you need to cool out, Markie says you're welcome to go down to his apartment. Cool out there in comfort. Would you like to do that?

Joey say no, he wait, wait for the man.

Then she remind him he did have to check in with his parole officer, make an appearance at the halfway house, lamentably, sleep there. She smiled, said, Pardon me, pardon us, but it's our responsibility. Markie wanted me to remind you. Part of the deal Markie made with the parole board to get you out.

Joey's gig at the halfway house was for something like thirty days or ninety days or a hundred and twenty days, he forgot now exactly how long, ninety days, and Markie's assistant wasn't sure either, some period of time until he became acclimated to life on the outside, but the production company, Markie, would eventually rent him some digs of his own, soon as the probationary period was over, ended, gladly do that, a place of his own, some solitude. No one connected with the show wanted him to feel like he was still in prison. He had the office right here where he could write, supposed to write, but he didn't have to write in his office if he didn't want or didn't feel comfortable, he could write wherever he damn well chose, she made that clear. He could write in Markie's apartment. In the subway. On a park bench. At Mickey D's. It was his call.

Wanna get laid? Markie asked Joey after he came storming in about two hours later, all apologetic. He said he had been on the set. There had been some problem. Nothing major. Numbers had come in. Overnights. The network were being pricks. Typical. He took Joey's hand, shook it, a power shake. Hugged him. They had met a number of times up at the lockup, Markie had come to visit. Then Markie push him away, stare in his eyes like there some kind of bond, grin, say, Hey, wanna get laid, dude? I can imagine, I know, a guy just getting out of the joint, you must be one horny son of a bitch.

Joey hadn't been with a woman in more than seventeen years. Probably longer than that if he thought about it, because him and Kimba had quit fucking at the end, before he done the dirty. They had been having their troubles that last year. They hadn't been what you'd call intimate at the end. Far from it. Not for a long time.

If Joey thought about it, he could get laid. To be with a woman, a real flesh-and-blood woman. He wouldn't need convincing. He'd like to taste a woman's cunt. Feel her warmth. But he hadn't really thought about it. Not like that. Not blunt like that.

Joey was sort of tired. Joey was sort of exhausted.

The scotch had gotten to him. He had finished the bottle, which was a fifth, but hadn't been quite full, so not so much, but enough.

He was feeling the scotch. His head was buzzing at the back of his skull, at the base of his neck, the scotch squeezing the head bones back there, twisting them upside his brain where the spinal column met the brain stem there, the medusa oblongata, whatever.

Real headache city like.

No fun. No fun for Joey.

She had a beautiful face.

The first time I ever saw her, man, I don't know what I saw.

I was dizzy. I was drunk.

I saw her.

I saw her.

I saw her spirit. Felt her warmth. Could smell her smell. I swear to God.

It was in Markie Mann's office, her husband's office. She had an office there somewhere too, in the complex.

He called her in on the interoffice to meet me, introduced us, introduced her as his wife, asked her if she wouldn't do him a favor, looking at me as he talked, hugging me, beaming at me like I was some prize pet, asking her if she wouldn't take me downtown to their place, get me settled.

She took my hand, smiled at me.

She said she'd be glad to.

Markie interrupted, said, By the way, we gonna have a party. We gonna have a party for you tonight at the pier.

I said, Okay, cool beans, a party. I'm into it.

Then we were in the limo, sitting side by side, going down Varick.

She said something, small talk, how was I feeling.

I said something back. Told her I was okay.

I groped for her name. I guess I hadn't quite caught it. I said Flora or something, called her something stupid.

She laughed, kidded me, said Flora was a horrible name, said her name was Fleur. Flower in French.

Flowers, I said.

I don't know why. I just said it.

Flowers.

She took my hand, squeezed it, said, I like that. She told me she was from Algeria by way of Marseilles. She said, I'm a writer too. And you know what? I been in jail too. Her hair short and very stiff and black and very well cut, the weight of it to the back, leaving her face open and exposed.

When she told me she'd been in jail, her eyes glistened, sparkled, her teeth shone. Her nose was crooked like it had been broke, her ears had split lobes where they'd been pierced and maybe the earrings torn out. She caught me looking at her, staring I guess, out of the corner of my eye, and she looked right at me, into my eyes, unashamed, not a challenge, but a challenge, and before I knew, she was back talking some shit about jail again and being what they call a beur, or whatnot, Arab spelled backwards in French or some shit, some disrespect in France, some kind of slur, but I show them, she laughed, I got them where it hurts. Fleur talking about her book, the book she wrote, and me thinking about something completely different, me thinking about pain, me thinking about sex, me thinking, ah, what the fuck, I be honest with you, this girl, this Fleur, this Flower, this woman sitting next to me, this Flowers, she so, she so, she so eminently fuckable.

O my brothers, what's gotten into me? So crass, so crude. How would she say? So déclassé. This Flower, this Markie Mann's wife, she was like sex incarnate for me.

And I was fucked.

And I knew it.

I knew it.

Later than it should be, everybody looking for me, everybody waiting for me at the party, on the pier. I be the guest of honor, but I ain't there. I'm late.

It's my history. I'm always late.

The limo apparently waiting and waiting to take me to the party, but I have to do what I have to do, take care of business. Go see the parole officer, check in at the halfway house, et cetera, et cetera.

Halfway house is like a men's shelter if you don't know, on East Third Street, no place you want to be.

So I never hook up with the limo for whatever reason and I walk over, through the streets, finally I make my appearance and there I am.

Oh, a lot of people there already.

People you know you know. People you recognize.

Hip crowd, beautiful people, a lot of familiar faces from magazines and the movies and TV, models, some kid magician with blue Ben Franklin glasses want in the worse way to make a dollar bill hang in the air and impress everybody.

Markie had me by the arm, escorting me around, introducing me. This is Joey One-Way. Joey, this is so-and-so.

You know.

Suddenly Flowers standing at my elbow, pressing my elbow to her chest, between her breasts ever so lightly.

Markie says, Joey, you know Fleur, right?

I look at her. Smile. She smile back at me.

Markie says, Fleur, you know Joey? Joey, Fleur, my wife. Her eyes in my eyes. You know what I'm saying. Her eyes IN my eyes, like she fucking me there, like she making love, her eyes to mine.

I said, Huh? What? Markie, man, you introduced us earlier this afternoon. She took me downtown.

He slap his head like so dumb.

Oh yeah, yeah. I'm so stupid, Markie says.

She was wearing a black dress. You could see into her cleavage. The black dress made her dark skin darker. Like I said, her hair was short, cut real blunt, real stylish, with this volume in the back, so you knew she wasn't no

American, and I liked the sweep of it, like you just wanted to fuck that. She had a crooked tooth. Piercing brown eyes. She's looking at me all this peculiar, real steadily, and loaded.

Sure, right, you know Fleur.

He put one arm around her, one arm around me. Like he owned the both of us.

So, you devil, he said. He punch my arm. How was she? How was the broad?

Earlier in the afternoon, when he come back from the set, he'd asked me if I wanted to get my rocks off, he could arrange, send over a prostitute.

I said she was great.

He grin, crack wise. He say, So, other than your genitalia, how's things going, boyo? Everybody behaving, saying all the right things to you?

You bet. Everybody very bolstering.

Fleur's eyes never leaving me. A real steady, appraising look, a dare.

Markie take his arm from around my shoulder, squeeze my arm, start walking me around the party again.

Fleur following behind a step or two.

Markie had hold of my arm, Fleur didn't have it.

Bobby, I want you to meet Joey. Joey, you know Bobby?

Bobby's the star of the show. *El Pistolero*. *El Pistolero Miami Vice* in New York. Bobby play a big man with a big gun. Bobby a big movie actor, deem it okay to slum on TV, doing it for Markie. He's the one Markie optioned my play for and all. Markie got a big plan. He's gonna produce the movie, direct it, Bobby star in it, me write it, between the lot of us, the whole kit and caboodle.

Bobby was sitting at a table in the corner. The big star whose name you would know if I named it. He had a drink and a cellular phone. The drink was in his hand, the phone on the tablecloth directly in front of him. The Ben Franklin—eyed magician was at the table with him, finally the dollar bill hanging suspended in the air just right. Bobby patted the seat next to him. He said, Sit down.

He asked me what it was like in the joint.

He wanted to know everything. If you said something, he would stop you and say, Did you say it like this? Or like this? It was like he was making a catalog for his acting, like a reference. Like this or like this?

People come over. They look at me. Nod. Then they bend down, whisper in Bobby's ear. They treat him almost like a godfather, and that's how he sits, in the corner, looking out, drinking his drink, his legs crossed, waiting for them to come over, kiss his hand, kiss his ass, whatever.

C'mon, man, let's move on. Markie grabs me, pulls me to my feet. Man's in demand, he says to Bobby by way of explanation. You don't mind, do you, boyo?

Right from the start, from the second I laid eyes on her, through the night and every night thereafter, to this night, every second, Fleur, she stick in my mind.

Every single second.

If you want to know the truth, all those girls, all those office assistants and production assistants and script girls and whatnot groupies, sticking around, talking at me, their long legs, their low-cut necklines, smelling sex. Still I was looking for her all night long, and without fail, when I spotted her across the room, she would invariably look up, invariably, and our eyes would lock and something would pass, something shoot at me, electric, every time. Under, over, through the crowd, our eyes would meet, like hungry, predatory, like love.

Markie tore me away from a bevy of twenty-two-year-old slacker models to introduce me to this couple. Special friends of his. The guy's a writer for the show. Staff writer. The woman takes my hand, tells me there's a connection between us, her and me, do I realize that?

No. No I don't.

Even to this day I don't know what it is exactly she was driving at. Something about my agent, who I'd never met, not even once. She said she was working on a set of some movie, and the agent was there, and he was talking about me, pitching me for some project. You're a very hot property, you know, she tells me. Yeah, right, Joey One-Way, you know, that mope wrote *White Man Black Hole*. Real hot prospect.

I talk to the writer for a few minutes. Guy graduated Yale, now he's writing cop show on TV. He says he comes from a long tradition, intellectual hacks, and laughs. I didn't get it. Then the writer who thinks he's a hack says excuse me, and exits for the bar, leaving me with his wife. She starts talking to me again, real intimate. She a blonde. Nice looking. Probably in her thirties, maybe older, if you looked hard enough you could sorta start seeing lines around the eyes and mouth. She talk very low like in a whisper, very sexy, and as she talk she moves closer and closer to me, till she got her face up-turned, buried in my neck, lips brushing my ear, talking some shit. I can smell her perfume, can feel her body, her nerves and muscles, and I'm drinking, feeling the alcohol, feeling all right, good even, and I'm thinking, man, why that guy run away from his wife like that, leave her with me, I mean do he know who he dealing with here, she right up there in my face.

I got to get away, man.

I'm feeling uneasy.

I mean I was tempted and everything. That's what I'm saying. All these girls and everything. This a woman here. I been away seventeen and a half fucking years. I don't know how to act.

Did I say earlier in the day Markie set me up with a whore so as I get laid? I told you that, right?

Oh man, the guy a solid. She was a firebrand, that one. Markie a solid.

So how could I wind up fucking him with his own wife, man? You hear what I'm saying?

Oh man, oh man.

Here's how it went down:

On paper, see, I got to stay in the halfway house every night. I can't sleep just anywhere, but, but he encourages me to use his apartment, get comfortable, get acclimated. Did I say that?

He lives in Tribeca, on Warren Street. Tribeca like this new neighborhood, Triangle Below Canal Street, didn't exist when I went away. Used to be all factories and warehouses and shit, now it's something else. Big spaces. All done up. Groovy. Very groovy.

It's not like I'm in the office thinking, Hey, Joey man, you out of the lockup, you home free, time to get yourself laid, and Markie sending me down there to his apartment do the dirty in his marriage bed. No, he genuine want me to see his place. He says, I want you to see what I done for myself, boyo, what's possible. Mi casa es su casa, and he hug me and kiss me and pat my back and punch my arm and say, Until you get one of your own.

Markie's apartment very she-she. It's all furnished very elegant and everything. It's a loft, like I say. With gleaming wooden floors and big clean windows.

He sends me down with his wife, with Flowers.

He say, Joey, this is my wife. This is Fleur. You heard me talk about her, right? Ain't she a peach, boyo? She's a writer just like you, you know. Her book was a big sensation, both here and in France. A regular international best-seller. Very salacious, that's what the *New York Times* called it, my friend. He kisses her.

From the start something was going on between Fleur and me, right from the start. She takes me down to the apartment, shows me Markie's setup, never taking her eyes off me, watching, watching, showing me how he got an office up front where the windows were and a audio-video system over here, a laser player, a 3DO, a black laptop computer with an active matrix color screen with nude girl screen saver, laser fax machine, the works. She looking at me, wink, says, Lasers be cool, no, *boyo?* and grin. Then out of the blue she comes close, smiles, measures herself against me, says I'm the perfect height for her, and step away.

She hand me the key, hold my hand two beats longer than she shoulda. She say lock up when I'm through.

We'd come downtown to their place in the limo, me and her, Markie he say he would have accompany us, but he don't want to gloat about his abundance of riches, and punch my arm again, let me know he just kidding.

Then after giving me the key, Fleur leave, no further question asked, she that much reluctant, distinct impression she don't really want to leave, and not two minutes later the bell rings, me thinking she changed her mind, she coming back, because I know deep down in my heart, deep down, she don't want to leave.

I says yes into the intercom.

A woman's voice says, I'm here.

I says, Who are you?

Mark Mann sent me.

I buzz her in.

She take the freight elevator up.

The door open, she come out.

She say, Hi, my name is Mo.

Irish chick.

Short for Maureen.

First thing I notice she got some beautiful set of knockers. Right off gorgeous tits. I see it's her asset, and she want you to know about it straight up. Not that she's been whipped by the ugly stick in other respects, because she hasn't. Far from it. She a comely girl with a spray of sweet freckles sprinkled across the bridge of her turn-up nose. But the knockers, man, the knockers, for a guy right out of the joint, and later, they in your hand they got a weight to them, they heavy.

I scared, I'm telling you, for whatever reason, I'm worrying, I'm thinking I don't know how much she like to fuck, you know what I'm saying? Like it's her job.

We get naked and she get me hard. She put spit on her hand like a ditch digger make herself wet.

I take her hand away from my cock. I say, No, I do that. Later you hold my nuts in your hand, I get myself off, but first I like to lick you pussy. Is that all right wit' you?

She shrug. She don't care. You the boss, sweet thing.

I suck on her pussy. She got a hairy pussy.

She clean. She smell so clean.

No question she washed her cunt before she come over to fuck me. I can smell the soap. The clean.

I pulled her up. I slid under her and I pulled her on top of me.

She was sitting on me, on my face, her clit right on my mouth. I was looking up.

Her tits hung down with their weight. Her nipples were not erect or anything, but they were pink and a little on the underneath side of the breast, so I could look up and see them perfect breasts and nipples silhouetted against the ceiling, her head back, arched, her hair hanging down her back, she a ginger hair girl, she moan.

I put my hands on her tits and I supported them, my thumbs on the nipples, and I felt the weight, so nice, and

I began to suck on her pussy.

I lick her clit.

I clamp my mouth on her cunt. To the whole top. I suck.

I'm so wet, she says. C'mon, honey.

She wants me inside her.

But for whatever reason, I say no.

I don't know why I say no, but I don't want to fuck. I'm afraid.

I say, Get me off with your mouth. But not right now, let me do this a little more.

I want to hear her come, man. I want to hear a woman come. I'm like dizzy with it. Maybe oxygen deprivation. I couldn't be harder on her cunt. I want to suffocate in it. Man, a woman, man. And I got the power. And she coming. And she coming. And she coming.

The thing about Joey, in his heart, he untrustworthy.

First day on the job, Joey working in his office. He had a script for *El Pistolero* in front of him. Markie Mann had scrawled on the top: Juice this.

Joey had looked at the script. He read the teaser. He didn't know how to juice it, didn't really even understand what juice it meant. To him it was already juiced. Juiced better than he could ever do.

Dialogue was good, real streetsy and hip.

Plot was clever, turned on itself, had required some thinking.

Tell you the truth, he wasn't able to even concentrate on it. He was thinking about Fleur.

Then his phone rang.

It was her.

She said, Do you know what a lemon is?

He thought that was some kind of weird quiz or test.

He said, Lemon? A fruit, right? A citrus. Grows on a tree. Yellow.

She say no. No, no, monsieur. She say *leman*, with an a. She say leman is a sweetheart or a lover.

She say, That's what I want to be with you.

Joey amazed, flattered, and very happy.

Next day she call again.

She say, You know how to use your E-mail?

Joey had lessons. First day in the office they send over a computer geek. He spend time with Joey. He sit down with him. He say, Joey, here's how to use your word processor. Here's how to use Movie Master. He say, Here's how to use your E-mail and your date book. Anything else you want to know, Joey?

Fleur say, Joey, I am going to send you E-mail. I send it to you, then you use the delete button. Don't leave what I send you on your computer. There are prying eyes here. This is meant for only you.

A few seconds later Joey's computer chime. A box appear in the right-hand corner of the screen. A quasihuman voice say, You have mail.

He click on the CCMail.

He click on the new-message icon.

The list come down.

One new message is listed.

Message from Fleur.

He click on it.

The message says, I am your leman. I am your leman hoyden.

Joey read the message and smile.

He read the message and think this is cool.

Joey want to reply.

He want to write something clever to Fleur.

Joey press reply icon.

Icon ask him what he want to say in response. He write, Anytime, anyplace, but, pardon my French, what the fuck's a hoyden, girl?

The response come back almost immediately. A hoyden is a tomboy, a high-spirited, sometimes-cocky girl, coolman.

He corroborate this. He take it upon himself to look these new words up in the dictionary. He have an American Heritage dictionary on his desk. He look up hoyden and it tell you how to pronounce the word (hoi'-duhn). It say hoyden is a noun. The rest just like she say.

He look up leman too, see if Fleur is right what she say.

She is right again. Fleur is right as rain.

So leman hoyden.

She want to be his leman hoyden, that's what she say, and he take her at her word.

The next day he get interoffice mail with two calendar leaves from one of those calendars has a new word every day, suppose to improve your vocabulary.

She attach a blue Post-it to the leaves. I want you to have these.

Fleur work at her English.

Fleur work and work.

Already she have basically no accent.

She say she always had a propensity for language. She speak six. Arabic, Berber, French, Spanish, English, and Italian.

Joey speak English, of a kind.

Joey look at the calendar leaves. One is for leman. One is for hoyden. The leaves tell you the definition of each, how to pronounce them. In the end Joey didn't have to have looked them up in the dictionary. He could have just waited.

Joey don't know why, but Joey pleased.

When Markie come in, he don't see the leaves. He say, So Joey, how about it, you juice it?

Joey say, Yeah, it juiced, boss.

The thing is, Flowers, I only really saw you that once. That one time at the music club. It was the very beginning. We still hadn't made love. You got the tickets. You called me, said Markie had something to do, couldn't make it, why don't you and me go. You were wearing that loose overall thing, so sexy. Isaac Mizrabi, or whatever, whoever the fuck it was. The music was playing. Baaba Maal. It was drums, man, Senegalese drums. We were on the balcony. You were sitting against the rail. I slipped my hand into your clothes, down into your pants. I felt your pubic hair for the first time, and just lay my finger on your cunt. I touched your clitoris. Just left my finger there on your clit. I put pressure there. Then I let up. I wanted you so bad, man. Pressure. Let up. Pressure. Let up. Then I let my hand do way up you. Two fingers. Three. You were so set. I knew what to do. You don't forget. The music was pounding. The beat. The beat. The beat, beat, beat. We were with the beat. Into the beat. Thump. Thump. The whole place rocking. Somebody passed me a joint. I smoked.

I passed it on to you. You took it. You smoked. You passed it back to me. I smoked again. I never stopped touching your cunt. Your cunt is juicy. Juicy juice, man.

I can taste it right now. Your smell. Your head began to loll. To fall. So slow and sensuous, languorous. You were moaning, man. Moaning soft. So soft. You looked up at me.

Your head had fallen. You looked up at me. I saw you. I saw you, Flowers. I saw you, right then and there.

What you didn't know, and I didn't tell you, not never, that whole time, getting hotter and hotter, people looking, into the music, looking, stealing glances, sex, man, but everybody, everybody into the music, into Baaba Maal, my hand up your clothes, down into your pants, in your underwear, touching your clit, this warmth, this wet. There was a woman, another woman, a woman behind me, a blonde, standing behind me, and she was touching me. I had never seen her before, didn't know who the fuck she was, touching me, touching my shoulder, my arm, my side, my head, my neck, the side of my face, from behind, me not seeing her. She was coming on to me, man, she was coming on. She saw you, she saw your swoon. She didn't see you like I saw you, but she saw you and she wanted some and she let me know I could have her if I wanted. Against the music, with the music, and she let me know it. Sex. So hot, Flowers. Sex in public. So fucking hot. I saw you, Flowers. I saw you that one time, really saw you.

You looked up at me. You were a little girl. I had no right. No right. No right to see you like that. My mind, man. What was I thinking?

I used to wonder what it would be like to actually be a good dad. A father. A real father. Not the shit I was. Any moke can shoot jack into a woman make a kid. But a father. A father to my girls. To my two girls. To be there for them. What I done to them, right? To be there for my daughters. To take responsibility. To take responsibility for something, man. I had absconded. I wasn't there for fuck all. For nobody.

I can't get into that, man.

Stay away from me, Flowers.

Don't touch me.

Nobody can see me.

Nobody can touch me.

Because of her.

Because of you.

Because of you, Flowers.

I'm sober.

Right now I'm sober.

The telephone is on my desk. It is one of those phones with hands-free mute, call-forwarding, Meridian mail, conference call. I look at the keypad.

I still remember the number by heart. The only thing that's different, they changed the area code. 718. Used to be 212. I know because I already tried to dial it. About twenty-eight times.

I look at the keypad. The numbers turn into a ballet in

front of my eyes. Or eye.

Did I tell you I only got one eye?

One window on the world.

I'm blind in the other. Born that way.

I tap the number out. 555–8316.

I don't know why, it's just there in my brain, it's just not a number I'll ever forget. Not even after seventeen-odd years. Probably be with me in there till the day I die. Me lying on my deathbed, Kim's mother's number buzzing in my head. Go figure.

Hello.

I don't say anything at first. I can't. My tongue or mouth or whatever ain't working.

Hello?

. . . Birdie?

Hello? Who's this?

Birds . . . it's me. It's Joey.

She hang up. I call back. Birds.

Silence. Silence from her end now.

Birds? You there?

What do you want? Scathing. Ungiving.

I just got out, Birds.

I heard.

Birds . . . I just . . . I just wanted to say . . .

There's nothing you can say. I don't want to talk to you.

I know you don't. I know. I just . . . I just . . . I just wanted you to know. You know, I loved her, Birds. I didn't mean to hurt her. I never meant to . . . hurt her . . . or kill her or nothing like that. I don't even remember. I don't even remember. I know that's no excuse. I . . .

I could hear her breathing. I could feel her wanting to hang up again, yet she didn't. There may have been some kind of softening. She just continued to breathe into the phone, waiting.

The truth be known, we liked each other. Even loved each other once. We had been close. Real close. She was always having Kim and me and the girls over for dinner. She always wanted to make what I liked. Pot roast and mashed potatoes and green peas was my favorite. Plenty of white bread with butter. Iced tea. I could always make her laugh. We sat around the kitchen table there in Brooklyn, laughing and laughing.

I always helped with the dishes afterward. Plenty of Sunday afternoons, sitting in the kitchen, laughing, watching Birds and Kim baking apple pies. The girls playing on the floor. All of us cracking up, giggling. Those were the good times.

What do you want, Joey?

I was looking for the girls. I just got out of prison and I wanted to see them. I don't want to get back in their lives or nothing. I don't want to cause them no pain. Nothing like that. I thought I could just look at them. I don't want to cause them no pain. I don't want to come between you guys.

You can't come between us, Joey. The girls have their own lives now. If they want to see you, I can't stop them. They have minds of their own, but they love me. I'm their nana and they come up with me, I brought them up, and I held them, and I reassured them when they were feeling bad, and they're young women now, so I guess if you give me your number I'll tell them you called, and if they want to call you and speak with you, they can. That's all I can do. I won't do no more.

Okay, Birds. I understand. Thanks. Thanks. I appreciate that.

You go on a journey in your head and you have to have confidence where you go and it is the hardest damn thing in the world to make that leap and to hope against hope that there actually something there. Some destination.

Joey is a lost soul.

If you want to know the truth, Kim was light, bright, and almost white.

He met her when she was eighteen and he was twenty. He was a busboy at the old South Street fish house

Sweets, at number 2 Fulton Street. He was the first white busboy they ever had.

Local 1, the waiters' union, was told to break the color line. Joey's father, who was a waiter and a union activist, brought him down when he heard there was a job open. He thought it would be good for Joey.

He pointed out a battered blue door on a shabby street. He said, In d'ere. Joey walked across the smelly street where his father pointed, through the mud and dirt and stinking fish.

In those days Sweets was run by a woman named Anna Pond. Her father had started at Sweets in 1847 when it first opened. He was a water boy. His job was to run down to the street, fill a pitcher at the public pump, run back upstairs, and fill all the glasses of all the diners.

Eventually the water boy took over the joint, bought it outright.

Maybe Joey's father hoped the same for Joey.

Anna Pond was ninety years old when Joey met her, when Joey walked in the door, climbed the steps. She worked harder than anybody in the joint, never stopped bustling around the floor.

She liked Joey right off the bat. Women were always liking Joey, taking him under their wing.

Anna Pond was no different.

She told Joey he might have a white skin, but he had a colored spirit.

One day toward the end of the lunch hour a group of photographers and models came upstairs. They'd been shooting a print ad at the fish market across South Street.

Kimba was with them, one of the models.

She was shy, thin as a rail.

Her teeth were buck.

Her forehead high.

Her eyes were brown, so was her skin.

Joey couldn't keep his eyes off of her.

The photographers took to Joey. Everybody took to Joey. Joey joked with them and kidded. Joey talked jive. Joey told the cooks to give their party the freshest fish, nothing but the best. In return before they left, one of the photographer reps took Joey aside, gave Joey a ticket to see Ike and Tina at the old Village East Theater. When he went there Kimba was in the seat next to him.

She said, Hi, don't I know you?

Joey, Joey.

Joey, Joey, Joey.

Joey made a terrible mistake.

Joey made a terrible mistake with Kimba.

The mistake, of course, was that he killed her, but the first mistake was that he married her.

In the old neighborhood, Joey heard this story. He knew it was true. It was about a guy who was doomed. He had gone to the doctor and the doctor had said, You're dead. He said, I seen a lot of people, but I never seen nobody abused their body like you. The guy was young, but he was a druggie, much self-abused, and the doc said he had the internal organs of an eighty-year-old.

There was these two brothers over on Ninth Street the doomed guy owed payback. He knew they were there, running at the mouth, saying how they fucked his old lady, how they had had her, and she was there for the having.

He went over to see them.

He said, Kev, Matt, you guys, you know, I'm gonna pay the price for what I done, for the life I led. They said, Yeah, Joey, waiting for him to get to the point. He said, I been into it, and I don't have no regrets, but I don't want to leave the life like that, don't want to leave the street, all loose ends, hard feelings. Understand? I want us to get over it, go out, you know, like friends, like the old pals we are, have us a time, bros.

So he the man and he go over to Seventh between B and C, his haunt, his treat, you know, where they chant C and D, coke and dope, hear the call, Feo, bajando, you know, and he cop, and he stop and he get a little battery acid he scraped off the battery of an abandoned car, hood sprung, its battery just there atilt, hanging down, leaking, and he mix that shit with the C and D, cut it into the coke and dope, and he go back to their crib, this Kev and Matt, these brothers think they're so wise, and they get off, man, they get off, and they feel the rush of the coke and the sweet hit of the dope, and then the acid hits them, and he laugh, this man, this guy, this Joey, who may not be Joey, he laugh, them getting all foamy, foamy in the mouth, you see what I'm saying, foamy, foamy.

Kev die right there on the spot in front of him, Joey pointing his finger at him, sucker, that's what you get for messing with me, but Matt chase him down the stairs, out to the street, and die there, right on the sidewalk, his head lying over the curb, over a pile of dog shit, someone didn't clean up after his dog.

Joey don't know what got into him. What he did or why.

He loved his wife. He loved her. But sometimes things get out of hand. Sometimes things just go and go.

Sometime Joey feel the violence in his life is the norm, not the aberration.

Sometime he feel life itself is the aberration. There is no norm. Did Joey say that to you already?

His wife didn't know.

Kimba didn't know.

Kimba never knew what she was messing with.

He was playing at love and so was she.

They was too young.

They loved each other, but they weren't equipped.

Men were on her.

She couldn't walk the street without being hit upon, he couldn't walk the street without smelling dope.

They had the two daughters and they loved them, but they didn't know.

Birdie tried to help. Joey's parents tried to help, but they were spinning. They were spinning and spinning.

Did Joey tell you he read her journal?

When she wasn't home, when she wasn't looking, when she was probably out fucking, he fought the impulse, but he couldn't resist and he sneaked it out from her closet, from her shelf, from under her underwear, and he read what she wrote. And what she wrote was not about him, but about fucking a guy with a freckle on his dick, who liked to put his finger up her ass, and it just drove him crazy. It drove him wild.

Did Joey tell you that?

Did Joey tell you how reading shit like that drive him crazy and how he couldn't control himself?

Did Joey tell you he went over there where the man with the freckle dick had an apartment on Tenth Street? Did he tell you first he had gone to his parents' apartment, got his father's gun he brought back from the Second World War out of his closet? Did Joey tell you he took the gun, smashed the ground-floor window with the butt, climbed inside the apartment, through the window? Did Joey tell you he pistol-whipped the boyfriend, made him cry, beg for his life on the floor, and shot Kimba? Did Joey tell you that?

Or did Joey tell you he can't remember, that he can't remember anything?

Joey's a walking aberration, a talking negation, Joey going, Please, baby, please, baby, please, baby. Please.

Joey got no way to go.

Joey is America.

Joey caught.

Joey caught in a web.

The web is here and the web is there.

Joey in the web. Joey on the Web. Joey on the World Wide Web. Joey on the Internet. Joey saying, Joey, you lose. Over and over again. Until it drum in his head. Joey

One-Way, you a one-way loser, dude.

Joey sit on his cot. Joey thinking. Joey thinking about his life. Joey's life is not boring. Fleur say, Joey, I never seen you bored. I never seen you ennui.

Joey think about that. Joey thinking about that right now. Right this minuto. Joey thinking about that sitting on his cot, tens of mens milling around, some eyeing him, some coming over. Don't I know you from the lockup, bro? Don't I know you from Dannemora? I seen you there, din't I?

Joey saying nothing, or if Joey feeling surly, him saying, Don't fraternize with me, bro. Don't be bothering me. The inquiring man looking hardass, his eyes narrow. He say, Look out, dude, no reason to be rude, dude. I'm just asking, d. When you get out and about? Everything cool? How you making it?

Joey saying nothing. Joey saying nothing, Joey dull-eyed stare. The pain behind his eye, the blind left, intense, him thinking of Fleur, him thinking of his father. Him thinking of times gone by by.

Bye-bye, dude.

Joey, man. Joey. O my brothers.

Joey.

Joey wasn't all innocent. Joey never was.

Joey remember one time he come home, Kimba's waiting for him. The babies in the other room asleep.

This was when everything was unraveled or unraveling.

She was waiting for him inside the door, maybe had been for hours, maybe just for minutes, maybe she had just heard him in the hall.

He put the key in the lock and turned it and opened the door and walked inside and just like that she kicked him in the balls. He went down to his knees.

She said, There, that's what you deserve.

She was right.

They took Apache wedding vows. Joey's father found the rings they exchanged on an almost empty R train, coming home from his four-to-four waiter's shift, four a.m., the end of his shift. It never occurred to him to ask the sleeping couple across the aisle if they had lost what he had found.

On the day of the wedding Joey got high.

Kim's cousin Dobbins brought some heroin, got off in the bathroom. Offered a shot to Joey. It was cool. Joey hadn't brought his works to his wedding. Dobbins had a set and they passed them around. What can Joey say?

Later Kim nailed him. She said, What are you doing, man?

There's no explanation, you know what I'm saying?

Joey shrugged.

She said, I can see you're pinned, man.

Joey smiled, nodded. Oh man, a junkie. But it was no surprise. She knew. Getting off at your own wedding. My oh my.

They wound up making love on the same bathroom floor where he shot up. Of course, he shot up sitting on the toilet. He fucked her on the floor, any which way he could get her, toss her.

He set her up on the bathtub to start. Picked her up physically and put her on the white porcelain tub edge. She was looking at him, her eyes wide, waiting. She had these brown eyes, wide and soft, silken, a little sanpaku, with the whites showing underneath the iris. He pulled up her wedding dress. Her mother had made it. White voile, white lace, with a cinch waist.

He pulled up the dress, pulled down her drawers, exposed her cunt. He kissed her twat. She moaned. Joey, she said.

She was wet right away.

She was always saying how wet she got for him. The bed sometimes was like a lake, overflowing with her juices, huge patches of wetness, seeping through to the mattress.

He touched the lips of her cunt with his fingertips while he licked her. They was a deeper brown than her skin, almost like a magenta. He spread her cunt and inserted his fingers. He kissed her in the soft folds. Her pubic hair was thick and wiry. The curls were tight.

She spread her legs more. Her feet were on the floor, her ass on the enamel. She put her hands, her fingers in his hair, behind his head, pulled his hair, his long curls. He bit her cunt, pulled her pubic hair back in gentle response to her pulling his hair, her cunt hair in his mouth, between his teeth, set his teeth, bit, caused her a little pain, cause he felt like that was what she wanted and deserved. Men and women, man. She moaned again.

Mmmm, like that.

Someone knocked on the door.

Yeah, Joey said.

Oh, the person on the other side said. Sorry.

Joey put his fingers in her cunt. Stood himself up. Set

his legs. He put both his hands in her, not the whole hands, but just the fingers, two fingers from each hand, in her cunt, probing, pulling, side to side, top to bottom. He stood up tall, arched his back, sucked in his stomach, and looked down at her. Her chin was up. Her neck sculpted. He liked the vision. His brown wife. She moaned some more. He turned her around, exposed her ass, tore his shirt out of his pants, loosened his belt, dropped his pants, his underwears, put his groin to her ass, pressed up, pulled back, took her from the back. Put his cock in her cunt, or she did. She guided Joey inside her.

He pumped a few times, maybe five times, maybe ten, but the heroin was in him, pulsing, working his blood and brain, and he couldn't really keep an erection. Maybe he thought about it, and that done him in. It's possible. You know how it is. She reached back between her legs, touched his balls. Sweet as could be. Just touched them like that, let them sit in the palm of her hand. Oh man, how good does it feel. Joey moaned, man, Joey moaned. And she moaned again. Mmmm. The erection came back.

Her ass was in front of him, her hips wide for such a slim-built girl. Her skin was the color of caramel, the white wedding dress riding up at her waist. He had his hands on her ass, and then cupped her breasts. He pulled down the dress to expose her white bra, then freed her breasts from the wire cups, had them in his palms, his thumbs on her nipples.

Come inside me, she said, more breath than voice.

All right, he said. All right.

Then she said, Give it to me. Give it to me, Joey. Give it to me.

When Joey went over his parents' apartment, tell his parents he was getting married to a black girl, they was upset.

His pops turned the color of hot pastrami and his moms said, Okay for you two, you make your own life, your life is your own, nobody's telling you what to do at this late date, but what am I going to say when you have children and I go to the supermarket with the baby and the checkout girl asks what is it? What do I say?

Joey didn't quite get it, didn't follow her. Didn't get where she was going with this.

He said, Mom, it's a baby. What are you going to say? We ain't intending to have no babies anyway, so I guess you're never going to have to deal with that question, now are you?

Then the twins come.

Come marching out.

Man, babies be babies. Black, brown, yellow, white, or no nevermind. Babies all got their charm. Babies all got their thing. Joey and Kim done two at once. Dark little things. Darker than Joey. Darker than Kim.

Little brown things with Caucasoid features.

Covered with slime. Multicolored umbilicus.

Nurse says, Want to cut 'em?

Doc turns to Joey.

Sure, Joey says. Cutting's my thing.

Neither baby was crying.

They was looking around. All alert. So this is the world. This is my father. Coming after me with a scissors.

They're very alert, the nurse says. Very.

Kim didn't do no drugs. She just toughed the birth out. She had this yoga breathing and it saw her through. She said all along pain was not what scared her.

Then what? What scares you?

It was a setup. Obviously, because she just looked at Joey and she said, You.

Joey cut the cords where they got them pinched off with one of them scissors you use for roach clips. Rheostats or whatever. Nurse point to the exact spot. You can't miss. You just cut. It's no big deal.

Did it twice. Once for each. Had a big smile.

Afterward nobody offered him to hold them.

They laid them on Kim's breast. She held them like that for a few minutes, the two cooing, looking at each other, with these navy blue dreamy eyes, her looking down at them, then they took them away for tests. We'll bring them back later, they said, like they thought we thought they was going to steal them away and never return.

Like they was going to be out on the street, screaming at the top of their lungs: Pickaninnies for sale! Pickaninnies! Get your red-hot, newborn pickaninnies!

Cheap.

Real cheap.

Dirt cheap.

They had put some drops in their eyes and shit like that, did some routine crap like that right there.

Kim had hold Joey's hand.

Kim reached up for Joey to kiss her.

Her hair was a matted mess. She looked exhausted, her eyes red-rimmed and bloodshot.

She looked like shit, but extremely happy.

Her lips were soft.

Her breath stale and delicious when he kissed her back.

Man, that's what love's about.

That's what love's got to do with it.

He loved her.

He always loved her.

He love her to this day.

He had a headache in his bad eye beat the band.

Oh man, oh man.

I been shot, man. Joey been shot.

The bullet come in, tore his pants, somehow missed everything else, all his plumbing, but left a little black hole through the crotch. Thank God he in one piece.

Joey had a vision once.

Joey dreamt he was sitting on a ledge. Underneath him was all these women. Their arms outstretched. They looked up at him. They was calling him, beckoning. They was saying, Joey, Joey. Come, Joey, come. That's a good boy. Don't worry. Don't worry, Joey. Come. Leap. Jump.

Joey don't remember what he done in his dream, leaped

or not.

There was nobody down there Joey recognized. They was all different types. Women, women, women. Women with their hair blowing free, women with babushkas and ball caps, women with veils and all kind of fruit shit on their head like Carmen Miranda. You know, there was a policewoman there too, and a female fire fighter, a girl jockey, all kinds of weird shit. In retrospect, now that Joey think about it, Joey think he remember seeing his shrink from the lockup, and maybe even this homeless woman he used to give dimes to. Maybe even his wife and his mother and his grandmother. Maybe even Fleur. Oh, there was all kinds of womens down there now that he think about it. Every kind of women, all eager for his bones.

Do you ever notice, O my brothers, that the girls on the street, the girls you see every day every which way passing you by, ever notice those girls, those young women are getting younger and younger? Younger and younger and more and more attractive. You ever notice that?

Maybe it's just a factor of age. I'm getting older and older. And more and more confused. So it's only natural . . .

It's a midlife crisis, pure and simple. Half your life is gone gone, maybe more.

Death is encrouching.

One night I'm sitting in a back booth at Cafe Tabac with Markie Mann and we're talking about my play, *White Man Black Hole*, which started out a prison production but went on to the B'way and won the New York Drama Circle Award for Best Play of the Year 1995, *White Man Black Hole*.

Markie optioned it for the movies before I got out and we're talking about his pal, the actor, whose name you would know if I named it, the star of his television show, *El Pistolero*, who I met at the party Markie threw for me, and Markie wants him to play in the movie *White Man Black Hole*, play me. And I'm not listening and Markie asks me what's the matter, so I start telling him how crazy I am, how women make me crazy, how Flowers make me crazy, although I'm not saying her name because Flowers is his wife and I'm fucking his wife and his wife is the one who's making me crazy, and I'm sort of giving him the rap in general, you know what I'm saying . . . women.

And he says, It's only pussy, man. It makes you crazy, man. Stay cool, man.

Flowers lying in bed with me, talking dirty to me, saying to me, I'll never let you go.

We was the same, Flowers and me. When we was together, joking around, comparing our anger.

What was we so angry about? I don't know. I don't know.

I had nothing to complain about. I was out of the lockup, I had money, I was living the charmed life.

And she?

She had nothing to complain about. She was in America, she was in the magazines, she was on everybody's lips, she was out of the lockup, she had money, she was living the charmed life.

Oh, man. Man oh man. All my torment. Most people probably just think, you just getting what you deserve, you dirty bastard Joey.

One night I'm listening to "Love Phone" on Z100, Dr. Judy, Jagger, a guy call up, he say, Dr. Judy, I got hair on my dick. She say, Hair on your dick? Where? Like in your pubic area or up the shaft? He say, the caller, No, no, no, Dr. Judy, you don't understand, I got HAIR! on my dick! I got it bad, Doc. It go up my shaft, all the way to the head, just so like the little pink tip peek out. Jagger laugh, he say, Dude, you got it right, you do got it bad, but she say, sympathetic, Dr. Judy, Hold the line, that's a problem easily remedied. I'll recommend you to my personal waxer. She the waxer of Madonna. That's how I got to her. Madonna recommended me to her. She great. You know, you go in, you say I sent you, you say you need your penis waxed. Just like that. She remove the hair. It hurt, but you be fine after that.

Me lying on my cot at the halfway, alone amidst a sea of men, listening, me thinking, how important Fleur say it was, she go for her bikini wax, she say, Joey, chéri, I want you be first one to see me. I want you see my wax before Mec, calling him her private name for Markie. Me saying, Yeah, I want to see you bikini wax, too, before Mec. Me thinking, man, it's his place to see her wax, not me. He her husband. She's Markie's wife. Not mine. Not my place. She's Markie's wife, man. I don't deserve no special treatment be first to see the wax, the red patch surround her crotch, where her pubes used to grow into the bikini line. I don't deserve none of that shit, you know what I'm saying? To be with her. She's Markie's wife.

But keeping Flowers straight is a trip, man. Flowers like a man. She fuck like a man. She think like a man. You don't want to be involved with Flowers, man.

Oh, man. Oh, man. I still thinking what it would be like to get off with my old works. The doojie's on me. I don't like none of those disposable needles that's all around now. Wasn't around like this when I went up to the joint, man. They was around, but they wasn't so prevalent. You could still get those old-fashioned kind, the ones the doctors cooked, sterilized. There was no AIDS. No HIV. It was just starting. There was other shit, but I never thought about it. Hepatitis. Got hepatitis once. Non A, non B. Wasn't too bad. Never suffered. Never turned yellow. I loved my old eyedropper with the baby nipple on the top, man, I keep that, I got it hid away at my mom's apartment. I cut out the center from this big fat book, slit the pages, made like a little coffin out of the guts. I think it was a book on grammar, something no one in their right mind would ever look into. Book like a tome. Tome like a tomb. Kept my works in it. My dope, the dropper, the rubber band, the nipple, the paper collar, the cotton. I like that shit. My gimmicks, man. The rubber on the baby nipple must be cracked and broken now. And you can't find that shit no more, that paraphernalia. Babies use different kinds of nipples these days from when my girls was infants. There's this one place I found that carried that old-style nipple, suce, is what it's called in French, man, what Fleur calls it. She turned me onto the place. Drugstore at Eighth Avenue and Nineteenth Street. She say, Baby, I got just what you want, sugar. She wants her baby be tough, be bad, have just what he want, give him options.

Options for what? Doojie don't offer Joey no options. Don't Fleur understand that?

On Twenty-third Street, right off Eighth Avenue, down the block from the Chelsea Hotel, there's this little bar, see? It's a bar I really like. Called Bar Blu.

One night this cat comes in there, see, sits down. In the corner there's this piano, it's been there for years. It's old. The sounding board's cracked. It buzzes. It's out of tune. No one ever plays it no more, hadn't for years. No, no one ever thought to. The guy who come in, he got long fingers, asks the bartender, You mind, can I play that? Bartender says, Be my guest. Guy with long fingers, this stranger, first time in the joint, sits down, starts to play. He plays beautifully. The music? The music is otherworldly, know what I'm saying? Otherworldly. Like from another planet. Everybody's astonished. Bartender goes over, says, Man, you got magic. You got the touch. Guy with long fingers, the piano man, his name is Joey, says, You think so? He says to the bartender, Hey, you mind I come in every once in a while, sit down, play for your customers? Bartender says, Mind? I insist! The bartender asks, By the way, what's the name of that song you just played? It was so lovely. Man looks him in the eye, says it's his own composition. I call it "I Want to Fuck You in the Ass, Come All Over Your Back." The bartender blinks, but he don't miss a beat. You got any others? he says. The piano man says, Yeah, sure, I got a million of 'em. He plays another. Even more beautiful than the first. Bartender asks, What's the name of that one? "All I Wanna Do Is Shove My Cock in Your Mouth So When I Shoot It Goes Up Your Nose." Bartender winces, says to the stranger, the piano man, the guy with the long fingers, Look, man, I love your stuff, but how about we keep the titles to ourselves, whaddya say? The guy with long fingers says, Sure, no problemo.

He starts the next Tuesday night. He's a sensation. The bar is jammed after that, people coming from far and wide to hear him play. One night a very attractive woman's sitting, listening. Maybe we know her. Maybe we don't. At any rate, she can't keep her eyes off him. When he finishes his set, she comes over to talk to him. She's beautiful, hot, sexy, maybe she got a hint of a foreign accent. Now that I think of it, it might even be Flowers, you know what I'm saying, it might even be her. But at any rate, like I said, this woman, or Flowers, or whoever, says, You play exquisitely, but do you know your fly's open and your dick's hanging out?

Know it? he says. I wrote it.

Bitch.

Whore.

Prostitute.

Cunt.

Fuck.

Fleur. My Fleur.

My Flowers.

Why you do it to me, Flowers?

Flowers.

Flowers?

Why you play me?

Why you play me?

Flowers.

So I'm sitting there, deep in the cushions of the hipster bar that is Cafe Tabac, coming back around, thinking, looking at Markie.

I thought if you was me, Markie, man, if you was me . . . him looking at me, all trusting, trying to figure it out, trying to figure me out, me knowing there's nothing to figure, nothing to figure, poor sap.

The late Cus D'Amato, the great prize-fight trainer who had Mike Tyson when he was a boy and young man, when he was just becoming Iron Mike, pontificated, No matter what a person says, what they do in the end is what they meant to do all along.

I believe that.

I believe that.

I accept responsibility for my own self. Did I say that?

It's so simple.

Justice so simple.

Joey want to talk frank with you. Joey want to talk how it is.

Joey don't want to pull no punches. Joey on a mission. Joey on a search. At the bottom, Joey want to be an honorable man. Joey want to understand honor and live honorable. He want to do the right thing, have standards. Joey want people to say, Joey One-Way, he a ace number-one cocksucker, but he an honorable cocksucker. Joey want people to say that.

Joey know.

Joey know from the git-go.

Joey know the city. Joey know the street. Joey know the culture. Joey know the game.

Joey been away a long time, but when he come back, you know what, not that much have change. Joey see the game and Joey know the game the same.

Joey always know that. Maybe people be hanging out, maybe their faces screwed up, or unshaven, sour in the mouth and tight in the nose, maybe their clothes are different, the way they dress, maybe their walks are something else, maybe they the sons and daughters of those who come before. But maybe not. Maybe not. Maybe they be the same, despite the years.

They the same motherfuckers.

The calls echoing down the street, down the avenue, the cries on the West Side and the East, maybe the bajando and the feo, maybe the guns, and the lack of knives, maybe the punches never thrown, maybe the boy in you face, twelve years old, standing chin to chin with you, saying, What you want today, man? What I do for you. Huh? What I do?

Not a whole lot of nothing, not change, in the increment of the cosmos, the cosmos the street, the smell, the drive, the noise, the headache, the march.

When Joey go to the lockup, the city he knew was up in flames. The big boulevard was a smoke screen, the fire burnt nightly, now he come back and there is cafés and there is restaurants, there is gallery and there is clubs. His girl take his hand, say, Come with me, baby, come with me, I know this after hours, we have fun.

What be with that, bro? Fun after hours. There is only one hour and that is always. It never end. The party go on.

It is confusing.

The intercom crackle. Joey, phone call, voice on the intercom say.

Clinique, he call one day. He call from upstate, from the lockup, from the public phone reserve for prisoners, he call Joey at the office of *El Pistolero* and he wait on the line when the receptionist say, Can you hold, and he wait on the line until she come back and say, Can I help you?

Yeah, you got a cat name Joey One-Way there?

Can I tell him who's calling?

You tell him it's the man. You tell him the man is calling on the telephone. He'll know. Joey know.

There is love and there is passion.

There is love and there is passion between men. Men is men. And their lovemaking . . .

. . . their lovemaking . . .

. . . can be brutal lovemaking.

And their lovemaking can be tough, tough-in-the-trenches lovemaking.

And their lovemaking can bring blood.

And their lovemaking can bring bruises.

And their lovemaking can bring anguish.

And their lovemaking can bring, surprise surprise, touch me gentle, asshole, and a blast of pain it bring, their lovemaking, bring you to your knees, and curses, too.

It can bring you pain, it can bring you to your knees, like I already said, their lovemaking, and it can bring your voice echoing against the stone, down the corridor, against the metal, against the flesh, it can bring you to the ground, to the ground, and below, below, way below, bitch, get down on your knees, bitch, get down on your haunches, bitch, because here it is, here it come, here's what I got, take it, you fuck, take it all. Take me. Take it. Take it all. Take it, you fuck. Take it, you bitch. Take it, you cocksucker. Take it. I'm giving it to you, and you taking it and you liking it, you better like it. Or else. O my brothers.

First time Clinique fuck Joey it pure power. Pure power.

It something between them. It something between men.

It unsaid.

It go unsaid.

And it better.

It better, sure as shit, go unsaid.

It one thing their lovemaking, then it another. Always the same for Joey. Nothing ever simple. Nothing ever straight up.

First time they met, first time they ever see each other, Clinique said, You better kill that man. You better not leave that man that way, you leave that man that way, he come back and kill you, so Joey go back and he do what have to be done, no questions asked, and no one ever the wiser, even those who seen, no one ever say nothing, 'cept how the man shit himself on his face, suffocate in his own feces and vomit, how he do that?, sort of remarkable when you think about it.

Joey remember he worry for a couple of weeks maybe they run DNA or some shit, some tests, but come to think of it, maybe DNA don't exist back then when Joey iced that dude, so what the fuck Joey worrying about anyway back then, maybe not DNA at all if it don't exist, maybe some snitch.

But Clinique, he's owed a lot of favors, have his own ideas, his own ulterior motives, how you say, lot of people owe Clinique, so it ain't surprising, no it's not, Joey wind up in Clinique's cell, and Clinique say, once Joey got there, moved in, Now, white boy, you kinda sexy, now you owe me.

What you gonna do for me, Clinique say, Clinique wants to know. What you gonna do for me, make up for what I done for you, what I know about you, what I'm not gonna tell.

You ain't a snitch, Joey says.

No, I'm not.

Then I don't owe you fuck all, do I? But if you change your mind, and you is a snitch, Joey says, then I find a way to deal with you. I don't care you the nigger here. I don't care you the toughest tough guy, the blackest black guy who ever come down the pike, I find a way or I is dead.

Tha's right.

That is right.

For bot' of us.

For both of us.

Tha's how it is.

That's how it is.

Couldn't say it better myself.

No, you couldn't.

Aw right.

All right.

They was friends. And they was what you call lovers. Of a sort. In the joint, man, no one has to know, and it is nature, and everyone knows. It's just the way it is, but they was both smart guys, and people needed them, and they bridged gaps, and they was serious, and they helped people, that was their philosophy. Clinique showed him. He showed Joey. Clinique been in lockup a long time. From the time he was still a boy and now he was a man. And Clinique, he taught Joey. There is a world in there which is unlike any other world, yet it is the world in its most pure and primitive state, and no one has to tell me, no one has to tell Joey, how it is done. And it is done with a kindness and with a caress and with using your head and saying what has to be said at the most opportune moments, and Joey was not above saying I love you to Clinique, to whomever, if it marched him on his way, and his way was one-way, Joey One-Way, and his way was out, by hook or by crook, his way was out.

Don't eat and run, Joey's mother said, don't tell tall tales in school.

Joey listen. Joey listen to his mama and Joey pay attention. Joey listen to Clinique's voice on the phone and pay attention.

So's what's happening? Joey says.

You don't sound like you feeling no pain, Clinique says.

Joey shrug. It's a whatso, he says. You wake up one morning, buddy, and you is delivered.

On his end, Clinique nod. Smile. He say, Yup, that's what I'm waiting for. To be delivered. Just like you, Joster. You think it's coming?

I think so, Joey says, as if he's truly thinking about it, truly considering. I really do, Clink. I really do.

Nah, Clinique says. Not for me, man. Me is someone different from you. You is a product of this country, bro. You ain't no nigger. No matter what you make yourself out to believe. You is the privileged class and I am the underclass. So be it.

So be it.

Joey had heard the rap before. Heard it more times than he care to remember, lock in an eight-by-four with this dude, longer than he care remember.

Remind me again, he says to Clinique, when did we become join-at-the-waist, asshole-to-belly-button victims?

Clinique laugh. I like you, Joey, he says. I always have. I told the girl who answered the phone you the man and you is, you is the man.

Joey have no argument. Him and Clinique have a rapport, always have, ever since that day in the shower room. Joey trying his best. Joey always try his best. Joey try never do no bad or Joey try his best never do nothing but bad. All according to when you talk to Joey. Know what I'm saying?

I been shot.

The bullet hit me in the face, drove me back against the wall.

Second caught me top of the head, near the crown, shattered my skull. Splattered my brains against the wall.

I manage to scream.

I scream, Stop! Stop! Why you doing this to me? Why you doing this?

Motherfucker.

Cocksucker.

Where you want me to start? At the beginning? There is no beginning. This is been going on and on. On and on forever. It's always been this. It's a loop. It go round and round.

I'm sitting at my desk and my boss comes in. I owe him everything. His name is Markie Mann and I'm in a love affair with his wife. He lays a piece of paper in front of me on my desk.

I glance down at what's written. They're words, like a poem.

What's this? I says.

Lyrics, he says. I hear it on TV, on the Conan show, transcribe it off the tube.

Cool, I says, looking it over. Who sing it?

Don't make no nevermind. Ruben Blades. Markie say it Spanish, Blah-des. I want you should make it into a script. Use the lyrics as a jumping-off point. Think you can handle that?

Sure, no problemente.

You're the best, boyo. The best. Loved what you did with that script. You walk the walk, you talk the talk. Keep up the good work.

You don't know what it is.

LIFE.

Life, you know.

Betrayal.

You try to comport yourself in a like manner.

Let me tell you something. This might sound funny, but this is the truth. I try to comport myself with honor.

I try to be an honorable person. It's not easy. Honor in this world. It's something else. There are forces afoot. You try to do your best. I'm trying.

I'm outta the lockup, and I'm fucked. I'm living with a bunch of other guys, guys on parole, mentally ill, homeless, guys fucked and fucking, sleeping with them, trying to keep my balance, trying to keep things in perspective, conduct myself well among these lost souls.

Markie instructed me, he says, Joey, you just go there, you go to the shelter, you do what you have to do. You make your appearance, you sign in, you sleep. But don't think about it. It's not you. It's like an outer-body experience. You'll be out of it soon enough. It'll be over. We're giving you enough bread, man. Pretty soon it'll all be over and you can pick up the pieces of your life. You'll have plenty money if you're smart. Okay? Okay, dude?

Okay.

If you're smart. Don't keep nothing valuable at that shelter, bub. They'll steal it from you.

At the shelter some old guy, looks like he should be my grandfather, not a bad-looking guy, but one worse for wear, maybe he don't have no teeth and somebody stole his dentures, asks me, You a prize fighter?

I look at him. Why you ask me?

Your face seems all broken up. You scarred all over, son.

I peer in the mirror.

We in the washroom.

Twenty sinks in a row.

Twenty urinals.

Twenty stalls.

I say, No. No. A prize fighter, no. Nothing like that. There ain't no prize to be fighting. Not me. No. Never was.

He touch me.

You skin so soft, tough guy.

I shove him away. Stay away from me, cocksucker.

I look back at the sheet on my desk. The lyric. The jumping-off point. It a piece. Start out:

A metal shark cuts into the night,
spilling the colors of the neon lights.
Pap, the hitman, is driving with his crew,
the Pérez boys. All born and raised in Barrio truth.
They're looking for a man
named "Sweet Tyrone."
In better days he was a friend
but is no more.
He broke the main rule that controls the street:
don't double-cross the ones you love, the ones you
    need.

Don't double-cross the ones you love.
Don't double-cross the ones you need.
'Cause you never know. 'Cause no one can say
when you'll need a friend out on the street.
Don't double-cross.

I look at Markie. Go back, look down, read on.

The metal shark parked across a downtown bar.
The barrio boys slid off the car.
The sawed-off shotguns pressed against their legs.
They're wearing raincoats and a dead-end face.
Inside the bar, the jukebox played a song
about a woman and a long lost love.
It's Friday night. The crowd is loose and loud.
It smells of piss, of beer and working clothes.
The boys went in behind the colors.

You translate this from the Spanish? I ask him.
    He sang it.
    In English?
    You heard of him? Ruben Blades?
    Yeah, I heard of him, but I thought he sang in his
mother tongue.
    He look at me, grin. He does. This is crossover.
Perfect for us.

"Sweet Tyrone" was on a corner, drinking rum and
    cokes,
holding a young girl he thought he owned.
When he saw the homeboys coming, he turned
and backed against the wall.
The girl broke off his last embrace and ran.
And before Tyrone could draw his gun,
two shotgun blasts ended his evening's fun.
In the bar, nobody turned around.
This part of town won't stand for clowns.

The barrio boys slowly walked and left the bar.
They slapped some high fives and got inside the car.
The girl came out and Papo paid her as agreed.
Into the night, they disappeared.
The street had spoken.
Don't double-cross the ones you love.
Don't double-cross the ones you need.
'Cause you never know. 'Cause no one can say
when you'll need a friend out on the street.
Don't double-cross.

So what you think?
Cool. Cool beans.

Joey can't fuck, man. All those years away. All those years dreaming. And Joey can't fuck. What's the matter with Joey, man? What's the matter with Joey? Why can't Joey fuck?

Joey can only get himself off.

All those years in lockup, man.

Joey can't fuck.

Joey says, Hang on, Flowers. Hang on, girl. Here we go.

Joey knows Joey.

Joey says, Tap my balls.

Like this?

Yeah, like that. Yeah.

Joey moans when he come. He moans small moans. To himself. He go: Huh. He go: Huh-huh. Joey go: Hmm. Huh-huh.

Joey can be very insecure. He can be very out front and very over the top, but he can be very insecure.

Joey worry he can't do Flowers right. He worry what he doing for Flowers. He worry how long Flowers gonna stick around if Joey can't fuck her proper. If Joey can't fuck her right.

Flowers been on the street. Flowers was a very young prostitute in Marseilles. She run away from her family, from her mother and father and brothers and sister in North Africa. Flowers a beur. She was a prostitute. You could buy her. You could buy Flowers. She was for sale. You paid your money and you had Flowers.

Or Flowers had you.

She wrote about it. She kept a diary. Flowers wrote about being a very young prostitute in Marseilles. She wrote about running away from her family, from her mother and father and brothers and sister. She wrote about the men. She wrote about being brutalized. She could be funny and cruel and right on the money.

She wrote a book call Profession: Prostituée.

Her book did well in France. It did better than well. It was published by some big French house and was widely promoted. Her picture was everywhere. Her picture was fetching. She look like a prostitute or a very young girl.

She says she was on television. She told me. She was on TV with this guy named Pivot who is like the Walter Cronkite of France. Pivot was quite taken with Flowers. On television she came across very well. With Pivot she was quite tantalizing. People took to her. Especially males. At the Frankfurt Book Fair, her publisher sold the American book rights to an American publisher for a considerable sum of money with the understanding that fetching Flowers would be available to do major promotion in the States.

After meeting her for cocktails, the American publisher considered it a given that she would have no trouble on the talk shows, Letterman, Conan O'Brien, Oprah, Ricki Lake. Flowers would have no trouble. Her English was honed, charming, endearing, and eminently sexy. Flowers was sexy. Sex sold. The American publisher knew that.

Joey walking on Eighth Street, left the halfway, gripped his jacket close at the neck, against the evening chill, even if it wasn't exactly cold, glanced at the scratched brass plaque, could have been for the first time, never before caught his eye, the sign not flashy, but a municipal afterthought type thing, New York State Bureau of Prisons Community Treatment Center, picked up his box cutter from where he stashed it every night in the weeds of the truck rental U-Haul lot on the corner of Bowery and Second, then doubled back, north, crossing

Bowery to Cooper Square, hang a left, where he remember Wanamaker's used to be when he was a boy, with his mother, shopping there on Saturday afternoon for socks, maybe mittens, get a upside-down ice cream cone at the cafeteria look like a clown face with little bit of peppermint eyes and nose and black licorice whip mouth.

Walking fast now, head down, already late for meeting Fleur, the streets full of people, night coming early now, the autumn rain cool, but pleasant in his eyes when he look up, him feeling like the end is near, like there is nothing left, if there ever was anything in the first place, who can tell, thank God for the city, the city giving him back something at least, making him feel whole, even when there was these tremendous gaps.

Everything was fucked up.

Everything is fucked up for Joey, in his mind, in the mess that is his mind.

No place for him out here, no place, the streets, the byways, the little hidey holes that make up this city and every city, every nook and enclave that he had ever known, sought refuge.

Joey don't want to feel bad the way he do. He don't need to. Joey don't want to be feeling bad for himself, diminished like he is, like there is no use, like there is struggle and there is nothing. Sometimes he feel like he be better off in the lockup, everything simpler there, less complicated and demanding. There was no moral choice in the lockup. He did the best he could, tried to stay sane, gave advice when it was asked, stay out of people's way. Helped those that asked for help. It seemed like so many people depended on Joey in the lockup. So many. That was the supreme irony because Joey could not help himself, never could.

You head is on straight, Joey, they would say. Keep it up.

And Joey would say, Yeah, right.

If you could see Joey now, glum, heading crosstown to rendezvous. If you could see him now. Wondering, worrying, thinking, ready. Ready to explode.

He look up.

Joey look up. Because he can feel it, he can feel it coming. Coming at him.

It's his sense.

A bunch of boys is hanging, standing against the parking meters, in front of the hair cutter's, hip-hop boys, white boys, twenty, twenty-two years of age, maybe they is pierced, maybe they is inked, Joey can't remember, their hats crooked, bullshit, one of them looking at him, watching him from a long way off, Joey picking it up, feeling his eyes on him, the way Joey do, the way Joey can always feel other people's eyes on him, the challenge, the boy saying when Joey get close, What you lookin' at, motherfucker?

Joey taken aback. Joey not going to let it rest like he know he should, Joey saying, You, you ugly little piece of shit.

The boy grinning, standing up straight now, pulling himself up now, ready he think, ready because it's not only him, but him and his posse against the world, he think.

Joey, before he know it, his hand in his pocket, his hand on the button of the cutter, pressing down and sliding the razor blade expose, before he know it, before he know what he doing, pulling the cutter out of his pocket, blade out, looking the boy in the face and backhand, one fell swoop, slashing, one clean slash, acrost the boy's pink cheek, acrost his cold red nose, deep to the bone, the crimson exploding onto Joey, red blood spraying Joey's face and jacket, and Joey barely stop, he just keep walking, not a hesitation, not a misstep, and Joey hear behind him a gulp and a cry and he hear, Hey, but Joey don't stop and Joey don't look back, Joey just keep going, the ugly little motherfucker, uglier now than he was before, uglier for life, Hey, what you looking at, you, you ugly little motherfucker.

Take that.

Take that.

Joey keep walking and he don't even wipe the boy's blood from his face where it sprayed him, where it rained and splattered, and he don't bother, he leave it on his jacket and his lips, and there is Fleur at the Papaya King at the corner of Sixth Avenue, in the window, at the counter, seeing him, her face brightening, she smiling, her white teeth, and the blood-red blood maybe it don't register on her, because, because, she don't say nothing, just kiss him, taste the blood, slide a hot dog from where she had two in front of her, one for her, one for him, Joey, baby, she kiss him, and the blood is on his lips, and on her lips, not even his blood, or hers, there is only justice, the blood of the boy, and she say, Hey, baby, and the blood on his jacket front too, and she say, Hey, baby, and now she say, You all right, sugar? What happened? Is this yours, in reference to the crimson, and he say, No, no, it ain't.

There's a lot Joey want to say. There's a lot he want to figure out.

Joey feel intimidated.

Why Joey feel intimidated? Joey a writer. Joey had a play on Broadway.

So don't talk to Joey, but Joey don't feel no writer.

Joey fuck up, Joey went to the lockup, Joey don't feel like no writer, Joey feel like an ex-con fucking up royally.

But he can't stop it.

Fleur called Joey interoffice. She all bubbly. She say as

how she and Mec were going to go to some hotshot reading, hear some eighty-year-old Nobel Prize–winning
poet read. But then something come up for a change and
Mec can't go, Joey want to go with her, be her date?

She come to his office, close his door behind her, sneak
a kiss, ask, so, is Joey coming?

She tease him, says how it's black tie, is he ready?

He blink. For whatever reason, the black tie part don't
strike him real funny, but make him feel real uncomfort-
able.

He ask her she serious?

His eyes narrow when he ask her. He hold her eyes. He
wait and see how much what he can see in her eyes.

He look at her face steady until he relax and decide finally to let himself go, that there is nothing there that is
hidden, that is dangerous to him, that she don't mean no
harm or insult or injury, no evil intent.

She shrug, sense the test is over, smile, say no pressure,
if he want to go fine, if he don't, fine.

The bottom line was it wasn't like he had choice. Not
really. She had him. He knew it, and he feared that because he knew it, she knew it, and if she knew it, as he
feared, then she had power over him.

It wasn't that Joey didn't trust Fleur. He trusted her, but
Joey know things have the potential to change very
quickly. A little nuance here, a little nuance there, and
everything is different.

Joey was half waiting for the ax to fall.

Three quarters waiting.

So she dressed him up with some blackity-black fancy-pants clothes she got from somewhere, he didn't know where and he didn't ask and she didn't offer, and they hailed a cab and went uptown to the reading, Fleur all over him in the cab, she take his hand by the wrist and she put his hand up her dress in the cab, inside her underwear, place his hand on her cunt, she saying, I don't know what it is but I love your hand between my legs, and Joey feeling her cunt hair, gently tugging, her panties resting on the top of his hand, the back of his hand, Joey looking straight ahead, through the windshield, at the street, feeling and nodding and saying, Baby, yeah . . .

She direct the cabdriver to the Upper East Side, they get out of the cab, the time they get there Joey sniffing himself, smelling like a cunt.

She make her entrance to the library where the reading is being held, unperturbed, say hello, hi to a lot of people or at least more than him, who knows no one although she introduce him, Do you know Joey One-Way?, and there are some who know him already or know who he is by reputation, shake his hand, maybe, maybe reluctantly, and look at him and maybe, very definitely maybe they don't trust him.

Or they smell the cunt on him and to his surprise when he sit down with all the shush, shush, the poet turn out to be some old man, decrepit, looking out from the podium.

Joey didn't expect no old man. Joey forgot Fleur say the poet eighty year old. Don't ask Joey why, but Joey had a picture, he thought the poet was a younger man, hearty, a poet in his prime, not at the end of his life, he had a picture of such a man in his mind, a image, rugged for some reason, a poet, someone he think Clinique had mentioned, maybe even had a book of his with a picture, gleamed from the prison library, probably why Joey thought the poet a younger man, because if he remember the book correctly, it an old book, a paperback, dog-eared and much read, Joey maybe even had glanced at a line or two of the man's poetry, poem didn't hold him he didn't think, if he remembered correctly, didn't read the whole poem, no way, what the fuck he did, the poet, sappy sappy, writing, naive, sitting there in the audience listening, listening to the voice, thinking this poetry is soft, this poet soft, making Joey mad, angry, the guy stopping at some point looking up, the audience capti-vated, even if Joey wasn't, Joey hating everybody, every other person in the joint looking up adoringly, thinking the old guy the epitome of poetry in the modern culture and poetry as we know it, and the epitome of who knows what else, male intellectual sexuality and bravura, the old poet, blue watery eyed, intoning his poetry, a rhythmic cadence, and Joey sat there and he listened for a while till his attention wandered and his eyes went through the au-dience, looking at the manly writers, Fleur leaning over, her lips brushing the shell of his ear, touching his ear, telling him who is who as far as she knows, she says, re-galing him with bits of tales and gossip, this one tried to seduce her, that one put his hand on her breast . . . and she laugh at them, these manly men, who'd touched her arm or kissed her cheek or pressed their chests to her chest, these studs and intellects, writers in tuxedos, writers in black tie, big egos, powerful visions.

And don't forget what else Joey saw: the handsome women, the handsome women, women so handsome, so attractive, do something to Joey, in their low-cut evening dresses, showing their cleavage, their intelligence, their sex, and Joey thinking what's happening? How'd he lose touch?

Women. Women.

Since before women, Kimba, she was the one, but Fleur made him think he was a man when she touched his chest or his cock and he had something manly to excise, he's cocky, and he stood and he felt that cockiness and he felt a power, the same power, and such an overwhelming fear, and he listened to that old man read and his attention was called back by the man's incredible voice and twang, as it almost turned on itself, a pastiche, but not quite, he saved it and it was moving, if you want to know the truth, and if Joey in any way could have let himself go, but Joey couldn't and for whatever reason he found himself wondering how come some fuck like this eighty-year-old fuckhead poet, how come some fuck like that wasn't his fucking father.

J oey don't know why he react so bad.

Joey don't know why you can't take him nowhere.

Tell the truth, it never cross his mind why, not at first, then he just flip.

After the reading there was a reception with caviar and hors d'oeuvres.

Joey stood there amidst the black-tie and evening-dress, champagne-sipping literati, drinking beer out of a bottle, refuse a glass, and he say nothing. Fleur had his arm and she gripping it tight with both her hands, sort of hugging him to her, and he say nothing, nothing to no one, but she was all chattery chattery, standing there hugging his arm, being charming, laughing at this joke from this writer asshole, laughing at that innocent little sexual innuendo from that writer douche bag.

It never dawn on nobody Joey could be with a woman like Fleur. No one think Joey could be with her. Not in their wildest imaginings. Joey low class. Joey low rent. No way Joey could have hold on her, no right, not a girl like that. Not a woman like that. Joey evening window dressing for a woman like that, nothing more, to their eyes.

See Fleur. They all knew her. See her, see that, snick snick teeth, little French tart. See her? See her slum. See her slumming. She slumming again. A girl like that, she make a career out of slumming. She brought that ex-con, for whatever reason think he a writer. Ha. See Fleur. She leave her husband home. See her. She brought her own personal evening entertainment, her own personal pet, keep her busy, keep her amuse, give her something to do. But he ain't nothing, not that one, he not amusing. What he doing here with us? Among our kind. Why she bring him? What is he? He don't belong. He ain't nothing. Not that one. Not that boy. Not that Joey One-Way. He not good enough. No way.

That's how Joey feel.

Joey couldn't stand it. Joey ready to explode.

Joey left Fleur, he pulled his arm away, and he pulled on the beer as he walked, drain the beer, stalk out of the reception room, leave them all behind.

He standing by himself in the lobby, looking at a fish tank. In the fish tank are these goldfish. The goldfish fancy, have red bodies and black faces, like a mask. They looking out. They look like a gang ready to commit a heist. Looking at Joey from the water, waiting for Joey give the signal. Let's do it, boys. The fish, they got these long red feathery fins with black tips. The fins flutter in the water when the fish swim. The tank is large and the backdrop is like some classic Roman ruins with grottos and columns and some such itty-bitty steps, like a stair-case. There is a treasure chest with jewels and a pearl necklace spilling out and a few broken old columns on the bottom of the tank and they are green with algae, but it is not because the tank is dirty, only because it is effect. Joey is looking at the tank, air stone bubbling, treasure chest bubbling, looking at the black and gold fishes that look like crooks, and someone come up and stand behind him, Joey can feel the presence, but he don't turn, but he catch a glimpse, a reflection, in the glass, he know who it is, not by name, or maybe by name, he hate to admit he know who it is, man big reputation, thick man, one of the hot-shit writers, maybe the hottest-shit writer of them all, you hear what I'm saying?, the machismo man macho writer, the writer with the biggest rep, the biggest rep of them all, the writer all them other hot-shit writers consider is more hot shit than them, leader of the pack. All them hot-shit writers think they better than Joey, this writer the writer maybe who Fleur said had a huge crush on her, touched her breast, touched her pussy, tried to kiss her, ask her for an affair, a charity fuck, anything, five minutes alone with her, and the writer stand there for a second or two, maybe a minute, at his full height, chest puffed out, gut sucked in, and he study Joey and he study the fish tank and he say to Joey, You an aquarian?, something like that, and maybe the writer mean one thing, maybe he mean another, maybe he was innocent after all, didn't mean a thing, but Joey turn real cold and he say, No, I'm a Pisces, and the man laugh like Joey some kind of moron or some kind of nut and he look at Joey like Joey really something small and pathetic and he say, No, no, chuckling, he say, I mean, are you into aquariums, are you into fish?, and Joey hit him with the beer bottle, lay him right out with the beer bottle, smash him upside the head, man sink to his knees. Joey kick him in the stomach, smug bastard, the man go down on the floor gulping for air, his lips drinking for air like the fancy fishes in the tank.

After that Fleur come running, look at the guy on the floor, the side of his face bashed in and bleeding, look at Joey, take him by the arm, get him out of there.

On the sidewalk she say, You all right, baby, you okay?, and when he say he is, she shake her head, and finally she say, You want to get something to eat, baby?, and the doorman get them a cab, Fleur slip him a couple of bucks, and there quite a racket still going on behind them, people trying to help their fallen hero, people gawking, and she say to the driver, River Cafe.

Joey wear a hat. Did I say that? Joey wear a hat all the time. What you call a stingy brim. Hat once belong to his father.

The maître d' ask Joey take off the hat before he come in the dining room and Joey almost get in another fist-fight, Fleur step in try to tell the maître d' he always wear the hat, the maître d' say he don't care, look at Joey, direct challenge, everybody testing Joey tonight, say rule of the house, no hat, take off the hat.

Joey say no.

Just like that.

Joey look the man in the eye, keep his expression under control, real neutral. Joey go to the bar. Fleur follow him, say, Baby, it's not worth it. Joey say, I be damned if I take off my hat, take off my hat for that man.

Fleur say, Joey, let it go.

Joey turn to the bartender, waiting for his drink order, Joey say, I drink what she drinking.

Bartender waits for her to say what she wants.

She drinking a martini with a olive.

The martinis in front of them. First thing Joey fish down, capture the green olive, eat the olive. He catch the bartender eye, ask, Could you give me some more olives?

The maître d' come back now, over now to the bar, say, Your table's ready, sir, but I'm serious, you've got to take off the hat. Without a word Joey take it off. Put the porkpie on his lap, squeeze the mustard-colored felt. He run his fingers through his hair. The maître d' say, You want me to take it, put it in the coatroom? He reach for it, Joey snatch it away, ready to punch him the man don't go away from him, Fleur say, No thanks, he keep it with him, he prefer it that way.

Damn straight.

Damn straight.

Joey One-Way.

The food is the kind of food, you know, drizzle on the plate. The restaurant is full. The best tables are on the river, overlooking the city. They sit in the third row from the water. The Brooklyn Bridge span the river just north of the dining room. Joey looking out. A little red-and-black tugboat cross the panorama, heading south to the harbor. Joey eat his food, terrine of confit or something, mallard or something, French shit, Fleur order, You'll like this, she says. Joey don't care, Joey so hot, Joey no company.

Fleur drain her martini, order a bottle of red wine, she don't consult Joey and the wine steward don't offer Joey no drink. He pop the cork, offer Fleur a taste, she sip it, nod, and the steward fill Joey's glass, then her's, Joey say, What beer you got in bottles?

Fleur sock him.

No way, she say, she going to let him drink beer. She make him drink wine. She make him eat the terrine or the confit or the whatever. She say, Ain't this good?, and Joey say, Yeah, it is, not grudgingly, because it is, but because he ornery, he *contraire*, like Mary Mary, you know, quite contrary, like that, just for the sake of it, but Fleur don't let him get away with it, and he like that, he guess, in the end, because in the end, some of that anger drain out of him, and he feeling better, and he got to admit the food is good.

He don't remember anything having a price on the menu, but that don't matter because he ain't paying anyway, she got Mec's credit card and it go on that, corporate account, bill the network, you a writer, ain't you, Joey, you work on the series, right?

Yeah, Joey a writer. Joey work on the series, if you can call it that, work, what he do. He sit in a room, he listen, he make a suggestion or two at the dialogue, spice that shit up, thataway, Joey. Juice it, baby. Juice it.

Now he suppose to be working on original teleplay, adaptation, "Shark cut into the night."

He don't know why. "Shark cut into the night."

Fleur waiting, waiting for him to say something, anything, him saying nothing, glaring out at the river, she finally saying, Joey? Joey, why are you so difficult?

Joey stay blank. Joey don't answer. Joey just glaring and glaring at the river, like the river is his enemy. Finally, Joey say, Baby. Joey finally say, Baby, look at me, man, Flowers, look at me. I am all fucked up. I can't go on like this anymore. I can't do this anymore. I can't. It's driving me crazy. You and Mec. I love you, baby. I love you. I can't go on. I got to end it. I got to walk away.

The cops made Joey afraid. It was irrational, but that's the way it played.

It Halloween and Joey afraid and there is a gauntlet of people in costume and they all so weird and young to Joey, so young and fucked-up looking and bizarre and staring.

They coming at him and they a coming and they don't stop. The streets is full of them and he is on the west side in the Village, walking down from the docks, walking first south, then east, first along Eighth Avenue, then cutting over on Horatio, angling east, east, east where the halfway is. Joey love to walk, Joey walk the streets of the city, because the city is his, is Joey's, and Joey is free now. He is free.

People talking at him. People he don't know. On the street they is talking and saying shit, and he ain't answering.

Happy Halloween!

Shit like that.

And there is people in his style.

Groups of them.

Castanet queens, gays in drag, going, Help, Officer. Help! Help!, going clickety-clack, and pink warnings posted, GAY BASHING BEWARE, and masked people balaclavaed, holding white balloons and kids even, infants, in strollers, howling, howling at the night, baying at the moon.

And it is a sad night. And it is quiet, despite all the noise and hoopla and hullabaloo.

And they is kids sleeping in doorways and on the street. Their faces painted white, white as death.

And they is looking up at him, asking, Got a quarter?, guys standing he knows, he swears, guys he's seen in the lockup, believe it or not, guys muttering, Smoke and dope, smoke and dope, their heads bent, their eyes averted, then fleeting, into Joey's eyes, Joey? Joey One-Way, don't I know you?

It is Halloween and Joey thought about a costume for a moment, for an instant, Joey thought about a costume, dressing up, when Fleur remind him, could be fun, and he think about it, he really do, think about a costume and what to wear, for the briefest moment, the briefest instant, could be fun, him thinking, Let it go. Let it go.

He think and think and he come up with nothing and that is why there are the people in his style, because it is Halloween and Joey have no style because he have no costume and his costume is himself and his disguise is no disguise, his hat pulled down over his eyes, hide his hair, still and all, he is exposed and all of them see him for who he is, the gauntlet, and this makes him scared and nervous and at Washington Square the cops is out and about and all around and there is barricades and fences and, You walk this way, this way, or you don't walk at all, Keep it moving, you hear what I say, what's a matter with you, man, walk, keep it moving. You hear what I say? What's up wit you?

All right. I'm moving.

You better.

Earlier, back in the office, Flowers touch his face, say, Hey, Joey, want to come with Mec and me tonight, party hardy?, and Joey say no, he can't handle it, being with Markie and her.

After he back off, after he say he can't see her anymore, and he know he can't not see her anymore, he suck her off right there on his desk, and Fleur, and no one suppose to know, the office kitty come up and he come to Joey's desk and he sit on the desk and he look at Joey and he smell him around the mouth like he smell the sex and he purr and he put his ass in Joey's face, real butch, and he flaunt his pussy ass, the cat's asshole and haunches in his face, and the pussy meow like Joey's suppose to do something to that ass, put his finger up the cat's rear end and get the thing off, Joey don't know what, the thing don't have no balls, he been cut, poor puss.

Markie come into Joey's office, the cat's ass in Joey's face, and Markie, Joey his pet project, and he sit himself down like he always do and he look at him, like he always look like he trying to look deep inside him, see what is to be seen, and he talk to him what it means to be a writer, all serious, and Clinique, on the phone from upstate, tell Joey about what's going down upstate, Joey knowing all too well he been there, done that, listen, listen good, Clinique saying, Learn your lesson well, blood, don't be coming back, because I ain't getting out, Clinique always wanting to do the same as Markie, talk to Joey about writing like it was God's gift, like it was something real, like it was a real gift, but writing ain't shit, writing a curse, Joey have no entitlement, no sir, writing the privilege of the privileged class, trying to go deep inside somewhere that is nowhere, where there is pain and confusion and nothing, nothing palpable or you can put your finger on, and Joey worry he never wrote, never could write, even *White Man Black Hole*, for Joey wrote in prison, whole bunch of prisoners pitching in, saying, No, man, Joey, that's not how you say it, man, it's said like this, everybody putting in their two cents, a good way of working for Joey, a safe way of working for Joey, free him up, free him right up, cause Joey don't know and it forced Joey up, Joey, who don't do good under pressure and it is Halloween and Joey's mind going every which way, can't nail down a thought, his only thinking them cops out in force ready to jump his bones and Joey can't go back to the halfway, and if he don't go back there, what if, and Joey walking the streets looking for something, waiting for something, searching out a face he want to see, an acknowledgment, his girls, that's who he's looking for, his daughters, trying to muster the courage like they would come out of the woodwork, or somehow Fleur, without Mec, coming up the avenue from the opposite direction and she see him and smile, light up his night, deliver him, someone please deliver him, from the evil that is parading every which way, the white faces, sharp fangs, vampire teeth, smeared black eyes, the ghouls, blood-red blood carefully dripping down pancake-white chins from blood-red rots.

C linique's mother saw the name Clinique on a jar in a house where she was cleaning, and liked it.

People called him Clink for short, had his whole life. The perfect irony, Clink wound up in the clink when he was sixteen years old for two murders on a street corner in East New York, Brooklyn, his old neighborhood.

It was a contract job, some kind of drug double-cross payback time, but the thing was when the double-crosser, this guy on the corner, went down, a four-year-old kid was killed too, the guy on the corner was holding the baby, his baby, and the execution went down anyway, the

shooters shooting through the little kid to get at their tar-
get, and according to him, to Clinique, him and his
brother, Olay, was the logical choice, the two biggest niggers on the block, so the cops just went after them, nevermind who really did it, made the cops' lives so much
simpler, wrapped the case up quick, and who cared?
Clinique and Olay? Their mother? The cops never gave
it or them a second thought. That was the reality of being
the biggest niggers on the block in East New York.

Olay was a year older than Clinique, and, according to
Clink, an inch taller.

I never seen him, although I'd read his letters. Clink
showed them to me. They came on a periodic basis. They
were both into letter writing. They both drew life without parole even though neither had been arrested before.
Olay was serving out at Attica. They was never, ever in
the same institution at the same time.

I asked after Clinique:

So you didn't do the crime?

I'm doing the time, so I must'a done the crime.

We looked at each other.

Eventually I told him about Kim, spilled my guts about
my brown wife, even though he never asked.

He listened, got all solemn, asked me why I done it.

I said I didn't remember killing her. I had only a vague
recollection. I remember beating the shit out of her lover,
pathetic little sunk-chest freckle-dick bastard that he was,
but I don't remember killing her.

He said, Didn't have nothing to do with her being a
Negro, did it?

There are guys in the lockup who couldn't live nowhere else. You know what I'm saying. They like it being incarcerated. Three meals a day, a clean well-lighted place, a bed to sleep, friends of a kind, plenty of enemies cut out your heart for a pittance, like a family.

It came around to eventually where Clink stepped in, made a proposition, I look out for him, he look out for me. Make both our lives easier.

He had respect.

He published the lockup newsletter, *Tales from the Crypt*. No one messed with him.

What Clink really was in love with was poetry.

Clink call himself a poet.

Poor naive, self-delusioned Clink.

You want to be my bitch or you want to be someone else's bitch, bitch?

Poor determined, self-educated, self-motivated Clink.

He wrote every day. His poetry was so bad. So bad. But it was his and it idled away the days for him and it gave him a sense of accomplishment, he took it really seriously, and it excited him, and every once in a while he hit it, I got to admit that. He would read it out loud to me in the yard or in our cell after he finished writing it. I didn't pull no punches, I shot from the hip, told him his writing was shit, but at the same time I never once discouraged him, I always encouraged him. Always said he was a lucky man to have what he had. He took a lot out of calling himself a poet, a writer, and doing it every day. Never forgetting it or letting it slip. There was nobody in that institution going to take that away from him.

A lot of men thought of him as a hero.

You want to be my bitch or you want to be some other asshole's bitch, bitch?

He said, How you fuck up your life so bad, Joster? How you do that?

He shook his head, said, Me, I didn't have no choice. The hand of destiny come down and whisk me away. But you, you a white man, you had everything going for you, and you act like an asshole, and look where you is. You is fucked and you is cooked and you is over. Lest you do something about it.

And what am I going to do? I says.

You can sit here and you can make a decision like I made a decision and you can decide you ain't going to let them have you, you can improve yourself and accomplish something.

He wanted me to start writing my own self.

He couldn't believe when I said I went to college, even if it was only general studies.

Didn't know what the fuck general studies was until I explained it to him. Community outreach.

Then he just grinned, whistled.

He said, College, man. He said, White man's college. He said, I can close my eyes and picture that. He said, I like that.

Kneel down, bitch.

What you do in that college, man?

I told him. I told him, Fuck all.

He recited his poetry to himself, nodding his head, repeating softly, his poetry, poetry, poetry.

Finally he come out of his reverie, come out of it, his music, look at me, raise his head to meet my eyes, his eyes dancing, glowing, says, So there is poetry and poetry is good.

So tell me again what you do in that college, those classes, man.

I told you, nothing. Not shit. I had a scholarship. I had no idea about anything. I was a lost soul, trying to get away from myself, trying to find out what was what, but I never found out.

No, he said, you found out how to be a drug addick and a murderer.

That's right.

Oh man, oh man, he said. You is one pathetic white boy. You be sitting there on top of the world, you had it made, the privileged class. You made it, you didn't even know it.

I knew it, I said. I knew it and I knew I didn't like it. I knew I didn't belong. I wasn't from their class. They didn't want me there. Don't you know people like us, we don't have no rights, Clink. We don't belong. The world's a rich man's game. Sure, every year they pick their one or two, their chosen people, but that ain't us. That ain't our fate. You don't get it, do you, you don't know nothing about social class? You a black man, look where you is, man. You don't belong in this world, there ain't no room in this world, not for you, not for me. That's the lesson I learned at fucking college.

Clink looked at me like I was crazy. Lucky you had your scholarship then, he said. Would have been a shame you have to pay for that shit, waste all that bread. His eyes was liquid and it was like through his eyes you could see into his brain and see the wheels and cogs working.

He said, You are an asshole, Joey. You know that. He said, They didn't let you into that college for nothing.

I said maybe.

He said, Why don't you start writing, quit wasting your time. Why don't you try write some poetry or something? Write some articles for the paper. It do you good. As it is, he said, you got the death penalty on you. He said, Your life here, right where you is, is a death penalty. Don't let them do that to you.

I don't remember the first time he kiss me, man.

It was bad business.

You so lonely. You so lonely you could die.

We was fucked.

You wind up in a situation like that, there's no out.

He push me against the wall, his anger welling, he said, You had a black bitch, man, now I got myself a white one.

I said, I could kill you, man.

He said, No you can't.

We come full circle. We go round and round.

He say, In the shower don't let that man do that to you, he come after you, he kill you, you leave it like that. At the same time protecting me, and I don't even know it.

I knew he was right and I went back.

I didn't run when the screws come. I stood my ground.

They say, What happened? Who did this?

I shrug.

Clink hadn't moved neither, he says, Man do it to himself, sir. He shit himself and choke up on his own vomit.

Screw looks at him. He shit himself on the face?

It's the damnedest thing, sir. Damnedest thing I ever done seen.

I'm a tough guy.

A tough guy.

A man's sexuality, it builds and builds. It comes upon him in a rush. I been away too long. Too long of my life has been spent in lockup, in isolation, to function normally.

Girl, you listening?

Fleur? I'm trying to figure this out.

When it starts up it's like search and destroy. You start up with me and you're automatically the enemy. Nobody else in sight, you're the enemy. You my searchlight, you my way out, you my threshold, my exit door. You the exit door.

What I want from you, Fleur? What I'm looking for? What do I have to lose?

It's like nothing. Nothing to lose. I kill. I'm a killer.

Don't try to stop me. Nothing out of bounds for me. I transgress all humanity and much of the animal kingdom.

I kill myself if necessary.

But I don't want to kill myself.

When I see a woman I don't think violence.

Believe me.

No. I think something else. I think sex. Something tender. That's what I think.

Fleur, for whatever reason, you bring me back to where I come from, my roots. I don't kill my roots. That ain't like me. My roots is all-important. My roots is who I am.

Let me tell you something.

When I was away I thought about it. I really did. All that time to yourself. All them years in the lockup, you got time to ponder. Time to consider. Nothing but.

A man kill his wife.

A man murder his wife.

Action speaks louder than words, ain't that what they say?

But what happened between me and Kimba, that was deeper than that, deeper than words, deeper than any action I might have taken. At least that's what I tell myself.

No, what happened between Kim and me was personal, down deep and dirty, just between us. It was love gone awry, it was love gone hellacious and haywire.

I loved her.

I loved my wife.

I still do.

I loved my Kimba.

I loved her then.

I love her now.

I got two daughters with her. We got two daughters of our own. Two daughters together. All grown up now.

Once we were responsible together and now I'm responsible alone.

A child transforms your life. Children transform your life.

My children transformed me. Maybe not for good and maybe not forever.

What made me get involved with Fleur? What drew me to her?

I knew it was wrong.

Flowers? I'm calling out to you. I need you, girl. Flowers?

You have a code.

You have a moral code.

You have a moral code and you try to keep to that code. For whatever good. For whatever good it does you. The worst thing you can do is you start thinking about it. You start wondering. A code got to be inside you to do you good. If you got to think about it and weigh it and ponder it, if you got to consider—*Am I doing right or am*

I doing wrong?—then it ain't no good. Then you already lost.

Everybody knows that. Everybody knows.

M
arkie Mann walk into Joey's office.

Sit down.

Sit down like he own the place.

Like he own Joey.

Joey, he says.

Joey look up, says, Yeah?

Markie ask Joey Joey have any ideas yet about the lyrics shark cut into the night, has he jotted down any thoughts he might have had, what happening, where it going, where it might go, *shark cut into the night.*

Joey shrug. Joey glare at Markie. Joey thinking he don't like Markie very much, justify what he doing with Markie's wife. The long and the short of it is Joey doing what he doing. He tell Markie he read over the lyrics a couple of times, mull them over, seem to him the story all there, within the confines of the lyrics that is, maybe he should hear the original song, Blades rendition, maybe give him some ideas, you know what I mean, he confused, what Markie want him to do, the story all there, right there, on the page, in the lyrics, what Markie want Joey to do exactly?

Markie say, You the writer, you tell me, boyo. That's what I'm paying you for, that's why I broke you out.

With a tone. Like Markie own Joey.

No man own Joey.

So go ahead, Joey, Markie says, tell me what you think.

I just did.

You just did what?

No one push Joey around. Joey a contrary spirit. Joey a contrarian. Like I said. Joey say, Whyn't you give it over to you other writers, you staff writers, you intellectual hack writers, why you need me? Like that. You don't need me.

Joey feeling something in his gut. Joey feeling something unsaid with Markie.

Joey have the guilt and the guilt color Joey's response, how he respond.

Still and all, Joey cut Markie some slack. Joey ease off. No reason to be snide or snotty with Markie. Joey think to himself Markie doing his job. That's all. Lot of responsibility sitting in the seat where Markie sit.

There tension in the room, across the desk, and they are both aware of it and into it and it is palpable. It is a palpable, thing, this tension between them, Joey One-Way and Markie Mann. After all, Joey in a love affair with Markie's wife, Joey fucking Markie's wife, and maybe Markie know it and maybe Markie not. Even though Joey think and pray it not.

Fleur.

Flowers.

The reality is, bottom line, Joey fucking the man.

Joey fucking Markie.

Joey fucking Markie with his wife.

Joey fucking Markie royally.

Joey fucking him and them.

Joey fucking him and them and all.

Sex with Fleur is crescendo. Instant crescendo for Joey One-Way.

He dream of her. He can close his eyes and feel her lips on his cock and he can see her dark eyes looking down at him, he can see her hair, and he can smell her cunt, her juices dripping in his mouth, and across the desk Markie be looking at him, and his look is inquiring and he is saying, Joey? Joey? Joey, you there? Joey, what the fuck?

Joey is that way. When you nail him down, when you put him on the spot, Joey's back go up and he see red and he is hard to fathom. His vengeance is real and it is palpable, like I say, O my brothers, like a red haze. Joey not to be reckoned with when he feel corner, like a wild animal, Joey is tough in the clinches, he across the desk and his eyes are dead, but his spirit alive, and he smell her cunt and he wipe his mouth and his nostrils twitch and he say, Yeah, here's what we do, Markie, shark, shark cross through the friggin' night.

Markie rush out of Joey's office to go to the set, he late, and not too long after, Fleur come in. She say, I got to talk to you, Joey. You want to go have a coffee with me?

Sure, he say. Sure. Why not?

They walk along the water, cut east on Twenty-third Street.

She say, Where do we go? And he say, You tell me, cool like, because the day before he was thinking once more, so hard, how he can't see her anymore, but already that's gone, he give that up.

She take his arm, say, Let's go to the Chelsea Hotel. I want you to rub your cock all over my face. I want to lay in bed with you and I want to look at you. I want to smell you. I want to hear the sound your cock makes as it slaps against my cheek. I want you to put your cock in my mouth and I want to suck you and I want to watch you come.

They walking and Joey thinking about her and feeling her presence next to him, full aware of her, the way she walk, the space she take up.

He can't help feel her, this flower, this Fleur. He can really feel her next to him, her energy or whatever, the vibe she putting out. Her aura.

She take his hand. They walking not too fast, but determined, like they know where they going through the cold, although they don't know where they going. They walking the streets of New York, and the city walking with them, right there with them, looking into the people's faces, the faces looking back at them, people looking at her through the vapor of their breath, sneaking their looks at her, or looking at her frankly, him thinking they thinking, what she doing with some ugly fuck like that?

Come here, she says, grabbing him by the lapels, pulling him to her, kissing him right there on the street in front of everybody. It's too far, she say. Where is that hotel?

Joey say he don't know, I think it's still a couple of blocks thataway. She say, Come in here. Let's go in here instead.

She drinking a coffee. I drinking a beer. It the Bar Blu. I look around, the dark, no one see us, we safe. We in the back of the bar, the dark bar, no one near us, no one even in this room. The waitress come in, say, Can I take your order?

We not eating. We just drinking, I say.

Fine with me.

On the table there is a salt shaker and a pepper shaker. There is a ashtray and packets of sugar and pink Sweet'n Low and blue Sweet'n Low, blue for boy, pink for girl, but I don't drink no Sweet'n Low.

Flowers don't take no sweetener in her coffee. She drink her coffee black.

The beer I drink is in a green bottle. I forget what brand. But I remember the feel of the bottle, the cold of it and the beads of perspiration, and I remember peeling the label while she talk to me.

The waitress come back.

You all right? Need anything else? Another beer, cowboy?

The conversation ain't started for real yet. Flowers ain't said what's on her mind.

She say, Joey?

I say, I just can't do this no more, Flowers. I can't.

She say she know.

A man with a goatee come by with a pair of shoes. He look in the back room, see us, then come in. Red and gray pumps, he say, For the lady. Give me what it's worth, brother.

In the face of the city, I am sitting in the back room of

a bar with a woman from Algeria. She a writer. She wrote a book about prostitution. Prostitution is something she have experience with, and that is good, because people say you should write about what you know. She write the book about her life. That is also good because she know about her life. She sit here in front of me, her coffee in front of her.

I say no thanks to the man with the goatee with the shoes that are red and gray pumps.

Flowers looking into my eyes in a very steady, even way, saying, Your cock in my mouth, your cock slapping against my forehead, rubbing against my eyes. I look back into her eyes and I feel my cock against them, I really do, and I try to keep up, I try to keep my eyes as steady and focused as she keeps her eyes. But I can't do it. I can't do it. I break off.

Don't worry, Joey, Fleur say. Don't worry about me. I can take care of myself. You don't have to feel guilty. As a matter of fact, Joey, I consider your concern for me an insult.

She put her hand on mine.

I'm not protecting you, Fleur.

No, you're not, she say. You're protecting yourself.

She says, Joey, I never meant this to happen. I never knew I was going to fall in love with you. It just happened. It just came over me.

Joey grunt, he say he know.

She say, Did it happen the same way for you?

I guess, he says. Yeah.

She like to talk writing with Joey. Everybody like to

talk writing with Joey.

I'm writing, she says. That's what I wanted to talk to you about. I'm writing a book in my mind. I hope you don't mind, baby. I'm writing a book about you.

It don't matter if Fleur wanted Joey to fall in love with her or not. It don't matter because if she wanted him to or not, now he is. Now he is in love with her.

There's nothing he can do. He can try to walk away, but he can't.

Mark me on this one, he tried to walk away, and he still trying, but he not strong enough.

Joey not strong enough to say he history.

So what Joey do?

Tell me.

Tell me what Joey to do, and I tell Joey.

Fleur say, Joey. Joey, I love you so much. She say, How we get involved like this? How we fuck up like this? She say, I take what I can of you, because I know I can't have it all.

Did I tell you Fleur has a child of her own? She and Markie have a child. A little girl.

Did I tell you that?

Markie a proud papa. Markie say, She the apple of my eye.

She eight months old. Fleur say Markie a very good father.

It her, she say. She not a very good mother.

She say she don't know, but when she look at her baby, she don't feel anything. She say, You'd think when I look at her I'd feel a bond or something, but no, there is nothing there. Even when she was born I felt completely separated. Isn't that weird?

She say she never wanted a child. It was Mec's idea. He wanted her stop taking the Pill. He said the Pill was dangerous and fuck up her body. He tell her he concerned about her because he love her. He tell her she should stop. She say no, but he throw away the packet that she keep in the medicine cabinet. She shrug like it no big deal, she say if it mean that much to him, so be it, okay. She say, Joey, you should have seen me when I was on the Pill, it made my tits like this.

Joey nod, smile. He don't exactly know how she want

him to react, what she want him to say. He not use to any of this. Joey in the dark. Joey like a dupe.

Fleur hold his gaze, tell him it only in America where men are so obsessed with women's breasts, do he know that? Fleur always trying to educate him. That very peculiar because Fleur much younger than Joey. Joey's life made Joey so old.

Fleur know the truth about Joey. She know how Joey like to make love. How he like to put his hand on her breast, cup her breast, and let his other hand hang and find its way between her legs and touch her clit and separate the lips of her cunt and feel the moist, the wet, and slip a finger inside her or let the tip of his pointer finger rest on her clit and press, just leave the pressure there, another finger, the middle, slip inside her, one finger, two, inside her, push up toward the clit, on the underside, find a spot, his other hand on her breast, cupping her, the nipple becoming hard against the palm, him looking down see the deep stain of the aureola, large and perfect, him lean over, his hand still inside her, his mouth find her nipple, he kiss her, he kiss her breast, touch the tip of her nipple with his tongue, run the circumference of the dark patch, she moan, he feel the spot inside her, he concentrate now on that, he feel so deep inside her and she moan. She moan. O my brothers.

SMACK IS BACK!

Joey read the headline. Joey stare at the headline.

Smack is back!

Just what Joey needs.

If smack is back, Joey scared shitless.

Joey weak. Joey know that. Joey know he weak. You won't get no argument from Joey.

It don't take too much for Joey to feel the pull of the smack, the pull of the street. That taste for the doojie never leave you, not really. It puts the fear of God in you, puts the humility in you to know how weak you really are. That the line is just there and you can cross over it so easy. And where do that leave you? How many people Joey know who is dead and buried now from that very pull? See the bodies? Nobody die beautiful from addiction ravage.

Fleur is doing that to him. Bringing him back. Back from where he came.

Joey is trying to figure it all out.

Joey is a good man. Deep down inside him, Joey a good man.

And because deep down inside Joey is a good man, Joey is always trying to figure it out.

The problem with figuring it out is figuring it out is always one step ahead of him.

Joey can talk to Markie. Markie can come in Joey's office and say, Joey, let's go out, grab a bite of lunch. They can sit down over tuna salad or a bologna sandwich or a hamburger. Markie can say, So how's it going, Joey? How you feeling? You okay?

And Joey can say, Everything's fine, Markie. Everything's okay. I'm okay.

No, really, how you doing? You adjusting, boyo? It can't be easy. You getting everything you need?

Markie all emotional and up front and right there and concerned and showing who he is deep in his soul and the horror of deception is washing over Joey, except the waves of it is like acid waves, not water waves, acid waves like burning him and torturing him and eating him away from the epidermis to the internal organs, and his bones is pitted and he pick up Markie's eyes, so imploring and earnest, and he hold them, hold his gaze, but then he can't look no more and Markie must think Joey's back on the smack or doing something fucked up, even if Joey say, Sure, guy, no problem.

Markie ain't leaving it there.

Joey, you know, I worry about you. To me you're like a brother, man. Not only did I put my name on the line for you with the parole board, bro, but I put my heart. My heart on the line. I'm in your corner, b. You're the one. You and me, we can go to the top. I can help you, but I don't make no bones about this, I'm counting on you to help me. So I got my own lookout invested in all this. I'm being up front with you, boyo.

Markie puts his hand on Joey's hand. Joey feels like pulling it away, it feels too much like some fag making a pass at another fag in some bar in the far West Village or on Eighth Avenue in Chelsea, you know, covering his hand, stroking it.

I want to, Markie. I want to, Joey say, pulling his hand away now. You know that, man. I'm not interested in fucking up. I'm not interested in going back to the lockup, that's for sure. I want to do the best I can. I'm trying. I am. Or at least I think I am.

Joey shrug, smile like he vulnerable and stupid and at Markie's mercy. Which in fact he is, bottom line.

Sure, I know that, boyo, Markie say. You're crispy, you're the shit, you really are, Joey. You're the man. Nobody can touch us when we're up there in the rarefied air. You got that?

Got it.

Joey wonder what Markie would be saying if he really knew what was happening, if he knew Joey was fucking Fleur. If Markie knew Joey and Fleur were having a love affair, if that's what you want to call what Joey and Fleur are having.

Joey and Fleur, they talk about it.

They have these long, heartfelt conversations. Conversations about their love, about their love for Markie, about betrayal, and doing the right thing and shit like that.

That's all they talk about.

Joey and Fleur, they wonder where they are, what they're doing, mutually professing, the both of them swearing to love Markie, not wanting to hurt Markie, telling how Markie saved each of their lives.

And maybe that's the point. They both owe Markie their lives. But neither is so ready for payback. The vig is too steep.

Or maybe Joey is with Fleur like an addiction and maybe that's weak. Like the heroin, Joey can't help it.

Dr. Judy says on the radio on Z100 that "Can't help it" is a "Love Phone" no-no.

Everybody can help it, Dr. Judy says. She say, Don't tell me you're having an affair with your boss's wife, but it's not your fault. You can't help it? Poor baby, of course you can help it. Who's in charge of yourself if not you? Of course it's your fault. Whose else fault is it? It's always your fault. Take responsibility. Take responsibility for your actions. There's always something you can do about it.

Think about it.

You can always walk away or turn your back. You can always be bigger than you are. You don't always have to give in to the flesh.

From where he's lying on his cot, Joey thinks about what Dr. Judy's saying all right.

What else is there to do?

He's always thinking Dr. Judy understand him, is talking directly to him across the airwaves. He imagines he's in her office, on the floor for some reason, on all fours. His naked ass is in the air and he's exposed. He's told her what he's got to tell her, and now he's waiting for his punishment, waiting to be fucked in the ass, and he wants it, he wants her to hurt him royally, and she's telling him, Dr. Judy is, You got a beautiful ass, Joey. I want to hurt you there and I want you to like it and come to your senses. I'm trying to help you. You with me on this?

Sometimes lying in the halfway, his cheap Sony mono radio, the single black plastic earpiece like a nipple plugged into his ear, Joey thinks how lost he is, how low. Joey wonders what's going to happen, but that's a lie, Joey knows. Joey knows what's going to happen. He can't sleep and he knows he has to tell Fleur once and for all that he can't go on.

Truth be told he's already told her that like ten times already, like twenty times. Or twice at any rate, or three times.

He says to Fleur, I can't do this no more, baby. It's not

like I don't love you. I do. I do love you, but Markie's my guy. Markie trusts me. Markie put everything on the line for me.

Fleur says she understands.

She says, Joey, I love you, too. That's what matters. I can't let you go. But if I have to I will. If that's what you want. Whatever you want, baby. I don't want to see you suffering. You've already suffered enough.

But the next day she's either in his office or on the phone or she's left him a message and he calls her back on the voice mail right away and leaves her a message too, saying he's sorry, and she's on the phone right back at him saying, I left you a message, baby. Did you get it?

Joey was like a guy in control, out of control.

Just trying to keep the women in his life straight in his head.

His daughters straight in his head.

Fleur.

Kimba.

Fleur slipping into his office. He putting on his coat. She say, Where you going?

A funeral, he say.

Oh, I'm so sorry! Whose?

My own.

One day Joey accidentally saw his daughters. They were sitting in a booth in the window of a restaurant on Sheridan Square in the Village. He knew they lived nearby there, right around there, in that neighborhood. He convinced himself it was them. It had to be them. It had to be, even though he hadn't seen them since they were four. Him and Fleur walking on Seventh Avenue up from Tribeca on their way to the Bar Blu, where they could be alone.

The two girls who had to be his daughters were sitting at a table in the window of a little luncheonette on Sheridan Square, and seeing them through the glass, like on a movie screen, the two girls, one laughing, one frowning, Vile and Bile, it had to be them, the Piss-off Twins, spitting images of Kimba, just like Joey remembered them when they was little girls, Joey lost all color, kept walking, said nothing, kept walking.

Then kept looking back, couldn't help it.

Fleur looked back too, had no idea what she was looking back at.

What's up?

Joey said nothing. Wouldn't divulge.

Don't tell me nothing, she said, something's bothering you. I can see it. I can feel it.

So after they'd walked another block, he told her.

She stopped in her tracks. Go back, she said. Go back, go in, say hello. Want me to do it? I'll do it? C'est facile.

No, he said.

The girls, the twins, his twins, they seemed so into themselves, they seemed so . . . Kimba-like . . . the two sides of her, he couldn't bring himself.

Still Fleur insisted and he reacted, blew up, screamed at her right there on the street to mind her own business, and she just walked away.

She didn't understand. Couldn't understand.

And he didn't try to explain, although after a couple of blocks he ran to catch up.

She turned to him. You are such an asshole, she said.

No I'm not, he said. I'm not an asshole.

There came a time when Joey could stand it no longer, when Joey was beside himself, and not cool, and his thoughts were veiled and oblique and horrible and overwhelming. There came a time when Joey felt he was not in control and he was out of control and he needed to see his daughters or he would die or he would kill and he in a moment of clarity which was not particularly clear at all decided he must see his daughters or else.

He had called Birdie and Birds had said finally she would do as she had promised, and pass his number over to his daughters, she relented and said she would do that although it was against her better judgment and against her wishes and against her being, Joey being the one who took her daughter in the first place, and to tell you the truth Joey did not blame her, not for a moment, he understood, but he tried to let her know that he was sorry, so sorry for what he had done, and he meant it, although he could not remember having done it, killed her daughter, he had killed her Kim, he had killed her beloved Kimba, and his beloved Kimba, he had killed her and he regretted having killed her, his first love, even though he couldn't remember, he couldn't remember killing his first love, that's the kind of state he had been in.

So there came a time and the phone in the office rang and he picked up the phone and he said, Yeah, Joey One-Way, and the voice on the other end said, Daddy?

There were two of them. They were twins. There were two of them, because when they were in their mother's womb the egg had split and from one there became two, and they were his and he hadn't seen them since they were four years old and they had been so close, two four-year-old adoring little girls wanting and needing their daddy, and their mommy, and he had betrayed them, he had killed their mother and by doing this he had taken himself away from them, and he had left them alone, although they had each other and they had their grandmother, who he knew was exemplary, but he had not so neatly removed himself from the picture, excised himself, he had ended the life of their mother and he had betrayed them and he had left them to themselves and now he was back and it was more than seventeen years since he'd seen them and he was back and one voice, not a girl's voice he once knew, but a woman's voice, a woman's voice was on the other end of the phone and the voice was saying, Daddy, and then a second voice, a clone of the first, said, Daddy, but the tone of the voices stopped him, because, if you want to know, the tone of both of them was dead.

Oh, man, Joey.

They told Joey it was okay. If he really wanted to see them, he could come up to visit. They said they had a small one-bedroom, west in the Village off Greenwich Avenue.

He rang the buzzer and the female voice on the intercom said, Who's there?, and he said, It's me.

They buzzed him in.

It was a walk-up.

There was a red aluminum snow shovel and a ice breaker, one of those square-bladed, long-handled deals, and a bag of rock salt left in the hall. There was a sheet of ice on the front stoop where the water was dripping off the fire escape from the sun or the eaves or somewhere up above, and for whatever reason, Joey had a vision of one of his girls, his beloved girls, did he dare think of them like that?, he never stopped, coming out of the building and slipping on the sheet of ice and flying down the stairs head over heels. So Joey, before he went upstairs, took it upon himself to reach for the ice breaker do his good deed, do something for his daughters, do something, and he went back outside and he broke up the ice with a vengeance, the sheet coming away from the brownstone stoop easily, more easily than he would have liked, in big clear chunks, and he swept that shit away and he spread some salt with his bare hand, and he did that before he went upstairs to face the two of them, his daughters who he hadn't seen in seventeen and a half years, his daughters, since they were four years old, his beloved daughters.

It's not easy to say how many times he had imagined the scene. He walk in the door, they all over him, they hug him and they kiss him and they say, Daddy, we missed you so much, and they say, We forgive you, Daddy, we forgive you for what you done, it wasn't your fault, you was fucked up, you was strung out, we know you loved Mama, we know you loved us, we forgive you, Daddy, we forgive you, we forgive you for what you done.

They was still four years old in his imagination.

But when the time come to climb the stairs, to go upstairs to their apartment and see them and be reunited, when it became time to go upstairs and accept their anger at him and their wrath and maybe if he was lucky their love, he could not do it.

He didn't know what it was, but he couldn't do it and he turned around and he walked away, back outside, down the steps, across the street, and into the shadows.

He stood in a doorway and he waited. He must have stood there for two hours, but eventually they come out.

There was nothing could have prepared him for what

he seen, there was no way. Because they was women. Two beautiful women. At their full height. They was lovely women, and he was ill-prepared.

He was stunned.

These women, these young women, standing in the winter sunlight, the daughters of his wife, the flesh of his flesh, was the same age of his wife when she died. Oh, man, that was the mind-fuck. Because he saw the two of them together, they opened the door, and come out on the stoop, where the ice and the snow no longer was, and the two of them was one and the one was Kimba, the two of them was Kimba, they was replicas, and he fell to his knees where he hid in the shadow and he began to sob to himself where he remained hidden, and he prayed to God, and he prayed to them, he said, Oh my babies, forgive me. Forgive me for what I done.

Later, in the twilight, the last light coming from the west, over the Hudson River, bathing the city in a pink and golden glow, the street, Joey remembering time gone by, Joey walking the streets, through the snow, Joey remembering walking with his daughters when they was little, trodding along, the two of them in their shimmery pink snowsuits, red mittens, and white boots.

Them taking the new snow off the garbage can lids. They saying, Daddy, this snow is so clean. Look how clean and white and pure this snow is.

Them taking the snow off the old and grimy and dirty garbage cans, putting it in their mouth, going, Yum.

Joey walking. Joey walking and walking.

Joey thinking. Joey thinking and thinking.

Joey thinking Joey is a danger.

Joey is dangerous.

Joey knowing disaster is just right over there.

Joey know given the chance in his heart Joey a good father.

Joey want to take care of his kids even though they grown up for always. Because through the haze Joey knew when they were young he was a good father, he tried, he really did, and nothing changed.

All I want is you, babies.

He imagined them hold out their arms, beckoning him, kiss them, hug them, hear them say, We love you, Papa, we love you.

No excuse, it was true Kimba could make him crazy.

Joey, man. Crazy fucking Joey.

Letting Kimba drive him stark raving mad crazy.

Fleur driving him stark raving mad crazy.

Joey had to do better. He really did.

Flowers says to him, Baby, they making love after spending the day in Coney Island, she says, *Tu m'excites quand tu fais ça.* She says, *Branle-toi. Suce-moi. Léche-moi. Suce-moi la chatte.*

While he coming she's whispering in his ear, she's saying shit to him in French. *J'aime te lécher les couilles.*

Shit like that.

Afterward, she teases him, says, It's a sex thing between us, isn't it? She says, It's something else, but it's a
sex thing and that's okay, isn't it, Joey? It's certainly okay
for you, isn't it?

She says, I love you so much.

She says, You are the love of my life.

It's a funny thing about Joey.

Joey lay there and he took it. When she said she loved
him, he knew he didn't deserve it, didn't deserve her love,
to be loved by her, but he took it and said, I love you,
back.

Before it happened, before everything fell apart the
first time, his daughters used to play this game with him.

They'd say, Whatsamatta?

And he'd say, Whatsamatta, whatsamatta?

It cracked everybody up.

Joey don't know.

Joey don't know whatsamatta.

Joey don't know a damn thing.

Joey scared he being played.

Everybody playing Joey.

Joey like a victim.

Joey don't take no responsibility.

Because Joey, you know, Joey ain't responsible, man.

Joey having a hard time with responsibility here, with
Who's liable for this? Who's liable for that?

Joey don't know.

Never did. Never did know.

Seeing the girls fucked him up royally. He didn't know what the fuck.

Walking the streets, looking for a fight, didn't matter with who.

Joey down and dirty tormenting himself.

Joey walking, Joey mumbling, Joey going over and over repeating to himself, Don't get killed, don't get arrested.

Joey going nuts.

Joey feeling the pressure.

Joey telling himself he can't see Fleur no more.

Everything too complicated.

Everything getting wrong.

Joey liked it when it was sweet and innocent, which, if you want to know the truth, was never.

Joey don't like complications.

Complications give Joey a headache.

He have a headache now.

Joey could take some Tylenol. But Joey scared of Tylenol.

Before Joey got out of jail, while he was still in the lockup, Joey saw a report on some television news show. The report said Tylenol, the headache drug, made people die. The report said Tylenol sometimes attacks the liver, can destroy the liver in a matter of days. Tylenol dangerous to people with a history of liver trouble.

Joey'd had liver trouble. Joey'd had hepatitis.

Joey had hepatitis that wasn't A and wasn't B. That's what the doctor said when Joey went to the doctor. Non A. Non B.

Joey wasn't feeling well. It was when he was a junkie and he was on the street, scoring on the street. He hadn't turned yellow or anything, his piss hadn't turned brown, his shit hadn't turned white, but his right side hurt something awful, and finally Kim took him to the doctor and the doctor did what he said was blood work, and the blood work came back to Joey and it said Joey had hepatitis that wasn't A and wasn't B. Doc said Kim should watch out too because it could be sexually transmitted, but her tests come back negative.

Later on Joey had a scare when he was in the joint. He had a pain in the side again, but this time it was on the other side, and he went to see the prison doc. The doc checked him out, and he asked Joey where was the pain Joey was feeling? Joey showed him. It was on the left side. Not a sharp one, but a dull one that never left him.

Doctor checked Joey out and he couldn't find anything. He said there wasn't much on the left side that could be giving Joey trouble. He offered, he said, We can do a blood work-up. The doc liked Joey.

When the tests came back they showed positive for hepatitis C. Doc said, We can put you on interferon. He said, It's an experimental drug, but I feel confident I can get you in a program. I know a guy doing research. It might save your life. The doc said, If you don't do it you'll be dead within the year.

Joey looked at the doc. Joey didn't feel like he'd be dead within a year. Joey felt okay. Except for the pain. That dull pain, eating away at his side, making him wince.

The doc was a handsome guy. He had black hair and an olive skin. He was tall and had excellent posture. The doc did a lot of AIDS and hepatitis B work in the penitentiary.

Joey had no reason to doubt the doc. But Joey didn't feel sick. Joey had this pain, like I said, but Joey didn't feel sick. Joey worked out in his cell and his body was pretty good considering all those years of abuse, pretty fuckin' strong. He did six to eight hundred sit-ups a day and a couple or three hundred push-ups. So Joey looked at the doc, studied him, and he said no thanks.

There was a guy in the lockup who did hands-on incantationary medicine. Joey went to him and the guy checked Joey out. The guy wasn't a doctor, but he was a healer. He had a gift. He felt here and he felt there. He said to Joey, You ain't sick. He said, There's this nerve that runs through your liver to the left side. He asked, Joey, did you hurt yourself in any way?

As a matter of fact Joey had hurt his knee. He was down on his knees doing something, you don't need to know what, and when it came time to get up, Joey had trouble. Joey had a real stiffness. For a couple of days or a week he was hobbling around.

The healer said, When you were hobbling you put strain on your side. You were walking this way and that put unusual strain on your infrastructure, and when you compensated that strain inflamed the nerve. The nerve gave a signal to the liver and that's why you're getting that fucked-up reading. But the liver ain't inflamed. I can feel it and it's not swollen or out of sort. That hepatitis you had, that's become part of your immune system. You're okay. You're not gonna die. Not yet, not from hepatitis anyway.

The healer said, Do some gentle stretching in your cell and deep breathing. In three weeks go back to the doctor, have him run the tests, they'll be negative.

And so they were.

But that don't change nothing. Joey still afraid. Joey afraid of his shadow. Joey don't want to die. And somehow, with Fleur, Joey smell death.

Joey and Fleur had a place they liked to go where you came in from the street and you climbed the stairs and asked to be seated or took a seat at the bar or at a small table, and they liked to sit in the back, where it was dark, and where there were flowers on the table and a candle burning in a small glass, the candle floating in clear water, and Fleur liked to touch the flame as the candle burnt, Joey touching her cunt under the table or sucking back beers, and the name of the place was, ironically, Flowers.

For whatever reason, Joey only drank beers in bottles.

If the waitress poured the beer before he told her not to, he wouldn't drink what she poured, he would only drink it from the bottle, where he liked to feel the glass and liked to hold the bottle to his lips, the cold beer, the hard round glass of the bottle, feel the round hard glass bottle in his hand, better than a beer glass or a stein or a flute or whatever the fuck they pour beer into these days.

Or any days.

Joey had a problem. Did I tell you that?

Joey had a problem.

The problem consumed Joey.

He tried to think of it and trace the start of it, although he didn't have to trace it so much, because it started right there in the joint, what a surprise, but he thought maybe it was only a symptom of the joint, localized to the joint, and would go away when he left the joint, but it didn't do that, the problem, it stayed with him, and he couldn't muscle it or finesse it or anything like that. It just was there and it had become part of him and when it manifested itself in the joint, who the fuck cared, but now that he was out, man, he wished he could get rid of it, know what I mean? Because the nature of the problem was Joey couldn't get hard. Or he could, but he couldn't keep it hard. It was like his focus had strayed sometime there in the middle of everything, or his blood had thinned or lessened or weakened or dissipated or whatever, and even when he was with Fleur he couldn't stay hard, and the nature of sex had changed for him, although Fleur wasn't complaining. She was always saying how sexy he was, watching him masturbate himself, him sitting on her pussy, his balls nestled in her muff, her finger up his asshole, or a bunch of her fingers up his asshole, just touching his balls, or touching his tits, or kissing his mouth, him jacking away, his finger straying to his mouth, touching the edge of his teeth, his lips, her going, Oh baby, so she didn't care, and he got her off, he could get her off with his mouth or his hand or his fingers, he put his whole hand inside her and she would moan, but she liked the pain and he could put his whole hand in her and lick her asshole and she liked that, but what she liked the best was him kissing her, kissing her mouth, and his finger just lightly touching her clit, she liked that, and he would kiss her and hug her and hold her breast and just touch her clit and she would get off like that in his arms, tight as could be to him, and that was sexy, and then he would get himself off, and he would come in her face or all over her chest and neck, and as it built he would moan, and it would come from deep inside him, and it was animal and she would look at him, and when their eyes met, she would smile, and he could imagine he could see deep inside her, into her, and he would imagine a love that she might have for him, and he would not be thinking clearly exactly, because he'd be working, jacking his joint, lost, working at it, and he could feel the come building from deep inside him, and she, she could feel his asshole tightening and she too could feel the come building, and that would get her off too, that would excite her, seeing him build to orgasm, feeling him build, and looking into his face, and she would say he was sexy, the sexiest man she had ever met, and she would tell him that, because she saw and felt his violence just under the surface, and he had almost raped her more than once, come close in some kind of ritual acting out of his violence and anger, as his frustration and anger had built, and he had almost torn her apart, but with his hand and not with his cock, he had tossed her, and he had choked her, and he had torn her clothes, and she had looked at him, and she had said, Go ahead, kill me, that's what she thought and felt, she thought, Joey might kill me, he might kill me, and she didn't care, she wanted to see how far he would take it, knowing he had killed before, and killed for love, she thought go ahead, if that's what you need, take it as far as you need to, and she looked up at him, and he didn't smile, he had a hardass cast to his expression, and his left eye, the blind one, went wonky, and he was a hardass and he was dangerous and that turned her on, him drinking beer out of a bottle at a table at the West Seventeenth Street bar called by his name for her, Flowers.

F leur looking at Joey, see him so miserable, still at the bar called Flowers, get all serious, quietly tell Joey if he so miserable she have the solution to all his problems.

Joey don't say nothing.

Fleur go on. Fleur say, if Joey as miserable as he look, she will leave Mec for him. Leave Mec for Joey. If that's what Joey want. It so simple.

She smile at him. He don't smile back. She shrug her shoulders, wait, wait for Joey.

But Joey don't respond, Joey don't answer. Joey don't

even look at her. Joey stare into space.

Fleur could wait and wait. Wait for Joey to say some-thing, for Joey to answer. But Joey not saying anything, Joey's answer not coming.

It's not like Joey hadn't thought about it. It's not like Joey hadn't wondered—being with Fleur all the time, living with Fleur, coming home to Fleur, calling out, say-ing, Hi, honey, I'm home. He had thought about it. Considered it. He had wondered.

Sure.

How could he help it?

It was more like it was the thing that was on his mind more than anything else, if you want to know the truth.

More than his self-pity.

More than his morose.

Joey and Fleur.

Fleur and Joey.

Living with Fleur full time.

Being with Fleur all the time.

Doing the dishes, bringing home the groceries, scrub-bing the toilet clean with a nylon brush.

The whole ball of wax.

Joey watching Fleur play with the wax from the candle.

Fleur leaving Markie for him.

Sure.

Why not?

Why not? The reasons are clear.

Fleur not leaving Markie for Joey. No way. Markie mean too much for her. Offer too much. Without Markie

Fleur back to square one. She nowhere.

The same go for Joey. Without Markie he nowhere, back in the joint.

Anyway, when he thought about her, about Fleur, try to imagine what it would be like, him and her, it always came back to him. Back to himself. Why that?

Maybe after everything was said and done, maybe all Joey could think about was Joey.

Sure, that was it.

But, you know what, Joey didn't think so. It was more like there were considerations is all.

So maybe Joey didn't love Fleur as much as he thought.

He looked up. Met her eyes. She was still looking at him, waiting. She smiled when their eyes met. He looked away.

Joey was a fatalist.

Joey believed shit happened.

Joey wished it was different, but he gave himself over to his fate, whatever that would be. Maybe this was a product of where Joey came from, his mother always repeating what she always repeated: This too will pass, day in, day out, This too will pass, no matter the particular crisis of the day, This too will pass.

That's how it was with Joey, that's how he thought. So when Fleur finally said, What about it, Joey, what do you want to do?, and she pushed, and she looked at him and she watched him and she waited for him, Joey eventually said, he said after a long time of silence, and nervous fidgeting, he said, What do I want to do? What do I want to do about what? Because when it was all said and done, what Joey thought really, what he really thought, was if he gave himself over to Fleur, if he gave himself over, she would eventually get tired of him and she would throw him over, and she would leave him and where would that leave Joey?

So maybe he had to beat her to it.

There's nothing Joey could do or say or what could he do or say anyway?

Joey.

Joey been shot.

Joey been shot every which way. He been fucked and he been shot and right now he sitting where he belong in his chair and he's thinking how it is with him and with him it is fucked and shot and fuckall too and he thinking about Fleur. He thinking about Flowers and what she offer and he thinking where he at. He ain't nowhere, but really where he is is back in his office and he been thinking about loving and he been thinking about violence and he been thinking about the dance loving and violence do together, then personalizing it and thinking about him and it and females and Flowers, what it is exactly he think he doing, and it ain't good and it is the very best of good and it is all confusing for Joey One-Way, which is just the way he like it, he guess, because it never been any other way but this way.

Which is when Markie Mann come in, because Joey in his office thinking these thoughts, sitting in front of his word processor, not writing or nothing, just playing, playing with the mouse, watching the cursor fly across the screen, fly across the script he'd written, now in production, for "Shark Cut Into the Night," and Markie Mann come in and he say to Joey, Man, we got trouble. Actor who play Sweet Tyrone, he want to rewrite his entire part. Simplify it.

Joey look up from his reverie, see Markie Mann. Joey a little stunned because Markie like the last person on Earth Joey want to see, Joey not really aware Markie Mann come in and sit down, but now here he is, sitting in front of him, looking worried, his brows knit.

Joey say, No sweat.

Joey say, What the fuck, who cares. Joey not caring. Not caring in the least about writing.

So Joey say it's cool. It cool. Don't sweat the small stuff. Let him do what he want. Man who play Tyrone Shore. Let us see what he come up with. What the fuck?

In response Markie say, It never let up, man. Trying to

allay whatever went down on the set, he say, Joey-man, it never stops, boyo. They never leave you alone.

I know, Joey say, and he ain't lying.

Same for you, right? Markie go on. It's a never-ending battle between truth, justice, and the American way. Right, Joey?

Markie looking to be reassured. It's the same for you. Right, Joey?

Joey pause, but eventually he say . . . Yeah, right, maybe.

Markie eyes get all weepy like he appreciate Joey giving him this one, like it make it so much easier for Markie.

In gratitude Markie say, Joey-man, anything I can do for you, man?

I'm not looking for nothing, Markie, Joey say. You don't got to do nothing for me. I'm cool. You liked the draft I done. That's all that's important to me. The rest is fuckall.

Ah, man, Markie say. It's always the same old, same old. It never fails. They take these great scripts and they just butcher them.

Who do?

The director, the actors, man. The usual suspects. I try to protect you, but you know everyone got their own personal agenda. Everyone got their different take. This one's trying to work out this and that, the other one's trying to work out this and that, you know, what's my motivation, what's my inner self. You know the drill. They all think they can write. I don't got to tell you. And the network. The network has its own fucking agenda. They never let up. They never give an inch. Your draft was great, man, but, you know, this is TV. This is writing by committee and we powerless against them. It's like you and me against the world, guy. I'm sorry. I tried. I really did. I love you, Joey. I love you.

I can take it, Joey says. I'm a big boy, Markie. They can't touch me.

But I know you care. I know you worked hard.

I didn't do nothing, man. I sit here. I type. The worst thing that happens to me my wrists hurt. I'm not in the lockup, I'm not upstate. I'm here. They can't touch me worse than I been touched. They don't live where I live and they never will. If this is what it takes, I can take it. It's easy, man. It's the easiest thing I've ever done. I'm cool.

Markie get up. He put out his hand. He say, I appreciate it. I really do. It's not everyone who takes it this well.

Joey says, Well, Markie, I'm not bullshitting you, this is how I feel. What can I tell you? If it turn out that bad, take my name off the credits. I could give a shit.

You don't mean that, Markie say, stroking Joey's head, smoothing his hair, playing with his curls. We won't have to do that. I promise. I'll have a look at it. If necessary, I'll tweak it. I'm looking out for you, boyo. You're a mensch, guy, you really are. You're my brother.

Yeah, some fucking brother. Some brother fuck his brother's wife. Yeah, that's a fine brother. That's what Joey do if he have a brother, he fuck his brother's wife, then he come in and kiss him on the lips and he say, Yeah,

man, we brothers, we solid and we up front and we for
always and always. Yeah, that's how it is for we, O my
brothers.

F leur had gone away.

Joey knew she was going away and it was okay with him.

She left the morning after she and Joey had spent one of the best nights they'd ever had together. Joey had gone with her to get her hair cut. He sat in a bar on the Upper East Side on Third Avenue waiting for her while she went upstairs to the haircutter's apartment. The bartender was a woman, a dyke, and while Fleur was upstairs they didn't have much conversation, but when Fleur come back with her new haircut, the bartender was sort of into Fleur, and got all talky talky, gushing about what a great haircut. Fleur flirted right back.

The haircutter was a dyke too and Fleur had been out dancing with her more than once. Fleur told Joey the haircutter was convinced Fleur was a dyke waiting to happen.

After a couple of drinks Fleur asked the bartender if there was a hotel nearby. The bartender winked, said, For you and me or you and him? Fleur threw her arm around Joey and said, For me and him, but maybe you get lucky next time. The bartender liked that. She said there was a nice hotel over on Seventy-eighth Street, off of Park. Joey and Fleur went over there, the night streets glistening and quiet. A young black man was sitting in the lobby, behind a sleek gray, very discreet Formica desk, with cut flowers in a small vase on the left-hand side. He handed them a key to a room on the seventh floor after Joey registered. The young black man asked, Your bags in the car? Joey said, No bags.

They went upstairs. The room had gauze netting over the bed and stainless-steel fixtures in the bathroom, a single rose on the nightstand. Fleur undressed for Joey and to his surprise he got hard right away. Fleur reached down and touched her clit, making tender circular motions until she was wet. Then she guided Joey inside her. She said, Oh baby, and Joey felt like he was going to come right away. He started to stop himself, but Fleur said, No, don't, I want you to come inside of me. She touched his balls and fingered his asshole. She could feel him swell inside her like he was reaching for her heart with his cock. She said, Oh baby, again and licked his upper lip and he came, moaning softly, not like the deep male growl she was used to hearing from him when he masturbated for her. She hugged him, kissed his lips softly, whispering to him, That was so sweet, and meaning it.

They went home by cab and she dropped Joey off on Third Street near the halfway, kissed him good-bye, then kissed him again and again, said, Talk to you tomorrow, sweetheart, or in a day or two, as soon as I get settled, I love you so much, and that was it.

The next day she left early to go out to Markie's summer house in Lloyd's Neck for a week, even though it was winter and the house had poor heat. Joey let the first day go by without trying to reach her, even though he was dying to talk to her, missed her voice, missed her. When he called a day later, she didn't pick up or wasn't home, and days went on and he called many more times but didn't get her. He couldn't understand where she could be, and he hoped she was all right, and he was dying for her to call him, but she didn't call, and he was getting nervous, like disaster was right there, and he fell into his solace, walking the city, wondering what was happening, was she sick, and out of the blue he began to feel the dope call, the doojie calling, calling his name. He began to imagine things, Fleur really ill or in trouble, and he called again, the phone ringing and ringing with no answer, and when a week was over she still hadn't come back, and he still hadn't heard from her, and his worry was beginning to eat him up, people at work noticing, saying, What's wrong, Joey?, and he couldn't say, I'm worried about Fleur, I haven't heard from her, and we're lovers, and it's not like her, and he had an overwhelming feeling of panic, and a feeling like the end was near, that the end was imminent, and then finally he heard Markie's assistant telling the receptionist that Fleur was back in town, but she had decided to give up her office and work at home, where she was feeling more comfortable and could spend more time with her daughter.

He called her right away and she answered, and it wasn't hard to pick up her tone, her distance from him, and when he said, Hey, how are you? she said so matter-of-factly, like she'd been practicing, It's over, Joey. It's over.

And he said, Excuse me? Excuse me, I don't think I'm hearing you right.

And she said, I'm sorry, Joey, I'm so sorry, but you don't understand, everything's changed.

And she was right. She was dead right. Because he didn't understand.

I s this what you want, Fleur? You want me to keep my rage under check? How you want me to do that? What does that mean, keep my rage under check? You don't want me to shoot you, is that what you mean? You don't want me to slice you, you don't want me to cut you?

I'm standing in front of you, girl. I'm six feet tall. I'm one hundred and sixty pounds. I got nine inches of cock and ten pounds of balls. What you gonna do about it?

You woman enough for me?

You gonna stand up to me?

You gonna show me how it's done?

I don't think so.

I don't think so, bitch. I don't think you got the chops. I don't think you got the balls.

You ain't shit, you know that?

You ain't shit, Fleur.

I got your number and your number come up zero.

You walking away from me, bitch?

You think so?

You don't know. You don't know who you messing with.

I'll get you for what you done to me. I'll get you bad and you'll regret it, you'll regret it forever and a day.

You hear me, bitch?

You hear me?

I want to be handcuffed to the bed, Fleur, your muff in my mouth, your finger up my ass, your whole hand up my ass, up to the elbow, impaling me, thick curly black hair pressed to my mouth and nose suffocating me, my throat constricting, no air, only desperation, horrible, searing pain, no recourse, nothing to do but take it, the pain and panic shooting up my ass to my cock, your hand on my cock, grabbing, holding, pumping. You looking in my eyes, your beautiful black eyes.

To Joey pussy a four-letter word.

When Fleur threw Joey over she denied him.

Don't you see that?

She denied him the opportunity to look at her one last time as a lover.

Joey standing in his daughters' apartment, over their bed. They're both asleep and he watching them.

He should have gone home long ago.

He shouldn't have been here in the first place.

No way he should be here.

He should be back at the halfway.

But he not.

Like I say, he here. Joey here. Joey watching his daughters sleep on a big iron bed. Joey watching them. He watching them sleep and sleep.

There are two bedrooms in the apartment, but tonight, they sleeping in one bed in one bedroom, and Joey imagine they were lonely or had nightmares, him remembering them when they were little and they would be scared in the night and scramble into one bed and hug each other and fall asleep in each other's arms.

He come up the fire escape. He break in their apartment, fit his box cutter between the double hung, slip the clamshell, silent as night, silent as death.

They stir, but they do not wake.

They both snoring, his daughters. Asleep in the bed, them not hugging. One facing one way, the other on her back, head thrown back. His daughters snoring. Little ins and outs of breath on the big iron bed, fluffy white pillows, smooth brown faces. Little noises of snore, peaceful breathing. And he watching them. He watching them sleep and snore and he listening to the intake and outtake of breath. He listening. Like he haven't since they were little girls. But they are not little girls now. They are big girls. And it is scary to look at them. Because there is wonder and there is desire and there is confusion when he look at them. What the nature of that desire is, Joey not sure. He don't think it is sexual, but there is an element of sex in it. Does it make him feel unclean? He don't know, because by nature he feel unclean. Joey in a state of confusion, like I say, looking at his daughters, his daughters who look like his wife, his wife who he loved and is dead, his wife who he killed, his daughters reminding him of her. Joey feeling the end is near. Joey feeling like the end, whatever that is, closing in on him.

Joey know he should go home, back to the halfway. But he can't. He can't bring himself to. He can't go home. He can't be in Fleur's arms. She's denied him that now.

So he stay and he sit there and he watch his daughters' sleep, maybe for the last time, their little intakes and out-takes of breath, no matter how painful it is, their lives.

Joey sitting at his desk for hours just staring into space. Nothing really coming into his mind. His mind a blank, his mind a haze. But not a red haze.

Joey feels like the beginning and end have come at the same time. All things being equal, nothing is equal.

Joey sitting and sitting and then Markie comes in and says, Hey, man, what's shaking? He says, Hey, man, you look glum. Whatsamatta? Wanna go over with me to the network screening room at five o'clock, see the video for "Shark Cut Into the Night"? You, me, Bobby, a few others, see how your genius played out. "Shark Cut into the Night." What you say, boyo?

About four-thirty Markie returns, says, I been thinking how about we walk over? I got a few things on my mind I need to talk to you about.

Joey get a cold feeling like Fleur spilled her guts to him, but Markie don't look like that is it, so Joey say okay, whatever.

The day before the phone had rung. Up until then he hadn't heard from Fleur, sure as hell hadn't seen her, and Joey was beside himself. He didn't know what the fuck to do. He'd felt like murder, he'd felt like death. Then the phone had rung and it was her, it was Fleur.

She said, I got to talk to you. I owe you an explanation, but I can't see you face-to-face.

She said, Joey, you have to understand. That time away with my daughter, I never loved you more than when I left. But you gotta believe me when I tell you what I tell you.

My daughter, my baby. You can understand that, can't you Joey? My beautiful daughter. I brought her out with me, I don't know why. I just felt I needed to spend some time with her. I felt like I owed her that much. You know how I felt so weird about her, like she'd come from another planet or something, but then one night I had cooked her dinner, and she was eating by herself, putting the food everywhere but in her mouth, and she put down the spoon and she looked at me, and I realized she has the same eyes as me, so black, and deep, and it was like looking into my own eyes and it spooked me and she looked at me and she said, *Maman*, the first intelligible word that had ever come out of her mouth, and I was amazed and she said, *Maman*, and I realized she needs me, needs her mother, needs her father too, more than I need you or you need me . . . Joey, do you understand?

Joey?

Joey walking the streets of the city with Markie, hurrying trying to keep up. Markie into it, really into it, walking the streets of the city with Joey One-Way, glowing, rising to a greater stature, to be able to walk the streets of the city with the man, strut the streets of the city with a down-and-dirty real-deal dude like Joey One-Way.

You okay? Markie says. You seem so troubled.

I'm okay.

Something's bugging you though, right?

If you say so.

You got the dope pull, boyo? If you do I understand. You know what, Joey, I haven't told nobody this, most of all not Fleur, but I been dabbling, baby. Just a taste here and there, but I been liking it. It's just like everybody says, it really takes the edge off.

Joey look at him, recalling the headline he had seen in the newspaper, SMACK IS BACK. Markie Mann doing dope, and proud of it, trying to impress Joey, show Joey how cool he is.

What do you want me to say, Markie?

I don't know. I don't know what I want from you, Joey, just tell me it's all right or something. I ain't been mainlining or anything like that, no skin popping, just snorting. Playing, like I say, taking the edge off, deliver me from myself.

Joey cool. He say, It's your life, patron. Ain't for me to say watch your ass. You're a big boy.

What about you, Joey, you ever get the dope pull? You must.

Joey look at him hard. No, Markie, no I don't.

In the screening room Joey settle into a plush seat. A seat that goes back, rocks, reclines, has plenty of legroom.

Joey close his eyes like this a way to shut the world out. The thing about Fleur, about what Fleur said, he does understand. He does. His own daughters. His own beautiful daughters. How couldn't he?

People come in. Some say hello. Bobby comes by, cuffs him on the back of the head. How they hanging?

Everything is everything, Joey mutter, not looking up at the big star.

When the tape come on, there is no credits or anything. The story have really nothing to do with the script Joey wrote. He barely recognize it. No two lines of consecutive dialogue the same.

But he look at it.

He look at it, fingering his box cutter, out of nervousness.

He watch.

Joey maintain some kind of detachment. Detachment, that's an easy thing for Joey. Detachment a state of mind. Joey got detachment down to perfection. No one touch him. It like Joey look at it, his work on the screen, and

Joey think, this have nothing to do with me, who the fuck cares.

After it over, no one seem to know or care if what they watched was any good.

Everybody on their feet congratulating one another. People come up to Joey, say, Excellent, excellent.

Joey want to cry.

Markie grabs him by the arm. Don't say anything, he says. Save it. C'mon, let's go get a drink, tell me all about it there. I want to know every one of your thoughts, b.

He takes Joey to a lap-dancing parlor on Walker Street. The girls are supposed to be better, more beautiful than they are. One is dancing with a pig.

Twenty bucks she'll dance on your lap, Markie tells him.

Joey says, Ain't worth it.

So what do you think? Markie says.

About what?

About the show, boyo, what I done to your script. Don't play games with me, Joey. Whaddya think?

It's fucking great, Joey says. Just fucking terrific! You really did a great job with the rewrite, you really got a way with words, Mec.

Joey knew right away, soon as the word came out of his mouth, that he had slipped.

Nobody called Markie Mec but Fleur.

Where'd you get that from? Markie says.

Where'd I get what? Play dumb. Don't admit to shit. Cardinal rule when caught with your pants down. Don't give nothing away. Joey reach in his pocket, feel his box cutter, finger it, play with it, slide the blade out and in, out and in.

Where'd you get that Mec shit from?

Where else, man? Flowers talk about you all the time. Ain't you her husband?

Flowers?

Markie nail him with an even more intense look. The look may be murderous. Joey think it is. Joey scrambling. He pull his box cutter out, finger it, play with it, slide the blade in and out, in and out, finally put it down on the table, rub his chin, the stubble.

You hanging a lot with my wife, are you, boyo? Markie says, eyeing the cutter, then Joey.

What is what is, but no, I'm not doing so much hanging. No more than anyone else, any other of her friends. But we talk a lot. We're a lot alike. You know that. We got a lot in common, and I see her sometimes. I'm sure she tells you. We're friends. I think she's great.

Yeah, she thinks you're the cat's meow, too.

Joey smile, trying to charm him, trying to disarm him. The cat's meow. I like that, Markie, Joey says.

What's a matter, you're not calling me Mec no more? So, let's get back to what's important, what do you think, Joey, you really think I did an airtight job on that fushtookanah script of yours? I thought I did a fuck of a good job my own self, but I just wanted to get it out in the open, see what you thought. Nothing behind your back, you know what I'm saying, boyo? I don't operate that way, I don't do a lot of shit behind people's backs, and I hope that's a little something we hold in common, not doing shit behind people's backs, fucking with what's another man's property, his wife, shit like that.

I ain't forgetting who you are, Markie, if that's what you're worrying about. I know what I owe you. I won't forget. It ain't me to fuck around like that. I'm a man and I expect to be treated that way. I respect that you're a man too.

Thanks, I appreciate that, Markie says.

He stood up and reached across the strip joint table, a naked girl on the stage shaking her titties, gyrating her twat, as he reached out to take Joey's hand, Markie's trademark power shake.

Joey took Markie's hand, tried his best to nod at him, smile.

Markie hesitated, then grab Joey, come around the little round table and hugged him tight, buried his face in Joey's chest, held him in his arms, like for the rest of his life.

So you dig my wife, huh? Markie says, pushing back to get a better look at Joey. You think she's really swell?

Markie was playing. Joey got that. It wasn't hard to see. Markie was doing his damnedest trying to get inside Joey's head, peer deep inside there, see what could be seen. He was trying to check out what was what with Joey. With Joey and Fleur.

Joey almost laughed, Markie was so fucking transparent. Joey sussed Markie out, scoped him, Markie waiting to see how Joey react, see if he can catch him, suss the real deal. If Joey smile, then it's all a big joke, a giant kid-around, but if Joey blanch, if Joey give back that fleeting eye, that little feral caught smile, that acrid waft of panic, then Markie knows and goes on the attack, because Markie must know now something up with Joey and Fleur, but Joey One-Way hope he too slick for him. He fucked up, but he pray to God he disguised it, and he ain't gonna fuck up worse than he already has, and when everything said and done, Joey will deny it to the death, and stick to his story, and when all is said and done, Markie finally push Joey away, kiss him full on the lips, say good night, clap his back hearty one last time, say, Brothers, we are brothers, and leave the club, go away into the night none the wiser Joey hopes, for what Joey done to him, but deep down Joey knows he caught.

After Markie gone, the dancing-with-pig-girl come up, say, Want a dance, sweet thing?

Joey say, No thanks, not tonight.

He reach for his box cutter, but it gone.

Junkies today, they seem to wear their addiction on their sleeves. Their tracks like a badge.

In my day we hid ours.

I gunned my wife down in a fit of jealous rage, and as a result didn't see the streets for a long time.

Because of it I lost my daughters.

My father died while I was in the penitentiary. My mother's incapacitated, home with a visiting nurse from the Medicaid. In the three months and twenty-three days I was out, I never once went over to see her.

Yeah, man, in my day it was three days in, one day out with the junk. That was the prescription, that was the way to keep your addiction in order. Yeah, we were all stronger, tougher, wiser, cooler than the next man in those days. Yeah, yeah, yeah.

Recidivism can take you back where you belong.

Aw, man, Joster, Clinique says, what you doing back in here?

The sounds men make. The grunts, the roars. The jungle sounds of men coming. The primitive sounds of men coming. Men ensconced in other men's assholes. Pretending it's cunts. Closing their eyes and pretending it's a woman, hearing her purr, and then to be shaken awake, out of it, out of reverie, to come awake, to hear the roar, to feel the hot flash of men's manly syrup.

It's me. It's me. I'm the one. I'm the guilty party. I'm the fuck-up. I'm the whoremonger. I'm the vestal virgin. I'm the indigenous party. I'm the fruit. I'm the ill.

They found Fleur's body on the floor in the bedroom of Markie's apartment. My box cutter with my fingerprints was under her. Her throat had been cut.

It didn't take a big leap for them to be coming after me.

My fingerprints were everywhere. Forensics found them on the bedside lamp, the headboard, the computer, the 3DO. Probably left them from the time I was there with the whore named Mo.

I made a mistake, all right? There's no denying that.

Joey made a mistake.

And for that he's paying the price.

We all pay the price, one way or the other.

But if I did it, man, I don't remember. I know I already said it about Kimba, but now I'm saying it about Fleur too. I don't remember. So shoot me. At any rate, what does it matter? She murdered. Fleur dead. My box cutter did the deed.

Fleur. My Fleur. My Flowers.

Fleur, you're dead, you're dead, baby, and I'm back in the lockup and this, this has turned from a fuck book into the sad, sad story of Joey One-Way.

Mec did me and you and us dirty. He come right out and he said it. He admitted it to me, but no one heard. It's all between the three of us.

Mec was your name for him, not mine.

Fleur, bottom line, you diminished yourself with me. I'm not good enough for you, never was. I'm not good enough. I let you down.

But you weren't good enough either.

None of us are.

Shouldn't I be ashamed? Ashamed of what I done, what I am, where I am, even if I didn't do what they said I done? I still done something.

I'm guilty.

I'm guilty of not being able to exist on any level in any society, except maybe in here, in the lockup.

I remember wanting to kill you, Fleur, wanting to feel the crush of your throat under my fingers. But it wasn't in me, it wasn't even in me the first time with Kimba, to take a mother away from her daughters, a mother away from her daughter.

I remember lying on my cot in the halfway, feeling in my pocket for my box cutter, realizing it wasn't there, remembering that I had lost it at the strip joint.

All I feel is pain and I can't get over that. I wish I could, but I can't. I can't get over it.

Every time I feel the pain, every time I feel the haze is about to disappear, it comes back.

I am the loser. I have lost.

Being dead ain't nothing, Flowers. Being alive is worse.

Fleur, why aren't you here with me? Why aren't you here right now? Why don't you walk through the cell door, sit down next to me on my bunk, tease me about my clothes, call me knucklehead, put your arm around me, look over my shoulder, try to read my notebook, sit on my lap with your legs spread, facing me, put my hand on your pussy, put my hands on your breasts, ask me, You okay, baby?, call me monsieur, ask me what I'm writing.

Flowers, why don't you walk through that fucking cell door right now?

Baby, it's not your fault.

Flowers, do you understand the love I hold for you?

What's the use?

I didn't do it.

I'm screaming from the rooftops. Does anybody hear me?

I swear to God, I'm innocent.

I'm innocent.

Baby, I didn't do it.

It was Mec. He framed me.

Did I tell you he put the moves on me? He wanted me to fuck him. I told him a man's sexuality in prison is one thing. On the outside it's another.

Why would I lie? All right, I've killed. I've killed more than once. I've killed and maybe I'll kill again.

Kill kill faster faster.

Help me, baby. Help me in my weakness.

Because, never again am I going to say I'm innocent, never again am I going to say I'm guilty.

I'm in and I'm out and I'm in.

Clinique come to my cell, put his arm around me, hug me. He say, It's all right, Joey. You're gonna make it. You're gonna make it, Joey-man. You the man, Joster. You the man.

The weather is turned.

Fleur, you know when it got hardest for me? It was once I said, Would it be crazy if I said I loved you?

Joey, man.

Joey.

Joey been shot.

Did I say that?

Joey been shot in the head, in the heart, twicet in the balls.

Doc says, It's all right, it's okay. Joey can still have kids.

O my brothers.

This is a conversation I heard in the halfway house.
It was the last thing I heard before the plainclothes cops
come down on me, say, Pardon us, sir, can we have a
word with you? I swear to God I heard it. It was between
a guy with no teeth and a guy high on bennies.

Guy with no teeth said, You know what happened to
me? I got hit by a bus.

Guy high on bennies wasn't paying much attention,
probably saw the plainclothes coppers closing in on me,
didn't know if they were coming for him or for me.

Did you hear me? the guy with no teeth said. I got hit
by a bus.

Guy high on bennies looked at the guy with no teeth,
then looked away, at me.

Couldn't a done much damage, he muttered, you're
still fucking alive.

Started in 1992 by Kevin Williamson, with help from established young authors Duncan McLean and Gordon Legge, Rebel Inc. magazine set out with the intention of promoting and publishing what was seen then as a new wave of young urban Scottish writers who were kicking back against the literary mainstream.

The Rebel Inc book imprint intends to develop the magazine ethos through publishing accessible as well as challenging texts aimed at extending the domain of counter-culture literature.

Below are some of the first titles to be published in the imprint.

Children of Albion Rovers - Irvine Welsh, Alan Warner, Gordon Legge, James Meek, Laura J. Hird, Paul Reekie
The bestselling collection of novellas from six of the best young writers to emerge from Scotland in the 90s
£8.99 - isbn 0 86241 705 8

Hunger - Knut Hamsun
A new translation by Sverre Lyngstad
with an introduction by Duncan Mclean
Classic first novel by the Nobel prize-winning Norwegian
£6.99 - isbn 0 86241 625 6

Young Adam - Alexander Trocchi
Introduced by John Pringle
Seminal first work from the Scottish Beat writer
£6.99 - isbn 0 86241 624 8

Drugs and the Party Line - Kevin Williamson
Introduction by Irvine Welsh
A polemic on the politics of recreational drug use
£4.99 - isbn 0 86241 647 7 - Available from June 1997

The Blind Owl - Sadegh Hedayat
Introduction by Alan Warner
Arguably the greatest Persian novel of the century
£6.99 - isbn 0 86241 676 0 - Available from May 1997

The above are available from all good book shops
or can be ordered directly from:

Canongate Books, 14 High Street, Edinburgh, EH1 1TE
Tel 0131 557 5111 Fax 0131 557 5211
email info@canongate.co.uk
website http://www.canongate.co.uk

All forms of payment are accepted and p&p is free to any address in the U.K. Please specify if you want to join the Rebel Inc. mailing list.